The Old Stonemason

The Old Stonemason

Karam Mishalani

Cedar Press

The Old Stonemason

First edition, January 2025
(second printing)

Editor: Doreen Martens
Book design: Adam Hay Studio, UK

Cover photograph: Karam Mishalani
Author's portrait: Rose Mishalani
Page 102. Karam Mishalani
Page 103. Ralf Franzen

Cedar Press
411 west 28 street
Durango, Colorado 81301
USA

Library of Congress Catalog-in-Publication Data
Mishalani, Karam.

LCCN 2024924305

Hardcover: ISBN 979-8-218-55542-9.
Paperback: ISBN 979-8-218-56566-4

BISAC Subject Headings:
FIC111000 (Fiction/World Literature/Middle East/General),
FIC043000 (Fiction/Coming of age),
FIC134000 (Fiction/Immigration).

Author's note

The Old Stonemason is listed in the category of historical fiction.
The popular and established norm for fiction storytelling today is
cinematic, with the catchphrase "Show don't tell."

However, I wrote the story the way my grandmother, the oral
history storyteller of the family would have relayed it to us.

While the story travels through the experience of the main
character, it also has the narration of cultural and historical facts
that give context to the events unfolding.

Philosophical and poetic observations and musings are
part of the story's fabric as well.

I hope you enjoy the journey of a life, once upon a time...

Contents

The ancient city by the sea

On an early summer day, Dimitri spent his 16th birthday with his cousins, friends and family along the rocky shores of Beirut's Pigeon Rocks. The two islands are both beautiful and severe, towering 200 feet above the Mediterranean Sea.

*　　*　　*

In an act of faith, love and joy of nature, Dimitri dived off the Beirut shore, into the waters of the rocky lagoon surrounding the iconic islands, timing his plunge carefully to make contact with the cresting swell before it retreated into the open sea, carrying him out with it. There he remained cheerfully buoyant while calling out to his cousins and friends, encouraging them to join him. When everyone was in, the friends swam out together to the islands.

It's a rite of passage for Beirut youth coming of age to swim out to the Pigeon Rocks and climb up the islands' streamlined striations before diving off the first level into the sea. Over the years, some ultimately graduate to diving off the very top during the annual cliff-diving exhibition and competition, an extravaganza eagerly awaited by Beirut's residents and tourists every summer.

As the sun began to dip towards the distant horizon, the sky blazed a deep orange hue over the shimmering Mediterranean Sea. Dimitri took his final dive of the day before emerging from the water to head back home with his cousins and friends.

Their youthful exuberance and seemingly endless energy harmonized with that of the playful *Sununu,* swallows that flew around them, zipping through the streets and alleys of the city as they chased and dodged each other, filling the air with their familiar chipping cheer-up calls and bubbly trills.

For Beirut residents, the *Sununu* have always been a welcome spring and summer visitor. Their remarkable flying abilities and playful antics are a joy to watch. It has long been considered good fortune to have swallows nesting in or around one's house.

Returning home, Dimitri was greeted affectionately by his grandmother, Teta, who proclaimed: "Today you have become the man of the house!" Lofty words for a 16-year-old with no father to hear from the matriarch of the family. And in the vast imagination of a teenager, it felt like being knighted by a queen, but better. It was Teta.

Dimitri's father died when he was four years old, heralding a time of sadness and hardship that his mother, Samira, handled with strength and grace, thanks to the support and love of her close-knit family. Teta moved in with her daughter and grandson and helped raise the boy while Samira ventured out into the brave new world of a 1960s career woman in the golden age of Beirut.

Beirut's golden age

The twentieth century saw a renaissance in the 5000 year continuously inhabited ancient city. Beirut became the educational, cultural, and publishing center of the middle East, with complete freedom of the press and more than 90 daily newspapers representing every political persuasion. Writers, poets, musicians and performers all gravitated to Beirut. Political exiles fleeing the latest coup or dictatorship in neighboring countries found refuge in Lebanon and a welcoming new home in its capital. A hospitable, socially liberal, educated, democratic city endowed with natural beauty became a magnet and playground for jetsetters from around the world.

Tourists would land at Beirut International Airport and be whisked away with great fanfare and hospitality to the hotel district overlooking the Mediterranean Sea. The Hotel Saint George, Phoenicia, Hilton, Normandy and a host of others operated at full capacity, surrounded by a thriving nightlife and lively music and theater scene that included seedy nightclubs and brothels.

For the well-heeled, there was an abundance of high-brow venues, including magnificent musical events held at one of the best-preserved Roman ruins in the world. The Temple of Bacchus in the Beqaa Valley is considered one of the finest examples of Roman architecture. European symphony orchestras, Russian ballet companies, American star Ella Fitzgerald, local Lebanese traditional dance troupes and the legendary Fairuz all performed on its ancient stage during the annual summer arts festival.

The Lebanese, with their reputation for liberalism and tolerance, were considered unusual in the region. They were thought of as traditional, rather than zealous or fanatical in their attitude towards religion and political ideology, and more interested in the enjoyable and practical aspects of life.

During this golden age, Lebanese philosopher Charles Malik became one of eight people chosen by the United Nations to help draft the UN Universal Declaration of Human Rights. It was to become the universal ideal shared by countries around the globe after the horrors of the Second World War. While the ideals have proved to be hard to implement, they reflect humanity's deeper hopes and aspirations for a more just, free and evolved world.

At a United Nations session in December 1948, Malik described Lebanon's unique role in the Middle East. "The history of my country for centuries," he said, "is precisely that of a small country struggling against all odds for the maintenance and strengthening of real freedom of thought and conscience. Innumerable persecuted minorities have found through the ages a most understanding haven in my country, so that the very basis of our existence is complete respect of differences of opinion and belief."

With this latest incarnation of the ancient city of Beirut, now newly independent, came freedom, progress and a cultural and economic boom.

Beirut's old masonry homes were traditionally built around a courtyard with a fresh-water fountain fed by the abundant wells under the city's rocky surface. Every summer, in the mountains high above the city, the snow-capped peaks of Mount Lebanon melt into crystalline water that makes its way through a myriad of springs, creeks and rivers flowing down to the coast, saturating the earth and filling Beirut's abundant wells and cisterns.

The traditional water fountains are surrounded by gardens filled with flowers, shrubs and trees and a designated seating area under a canopy of interwoven grapevines whose leaves give shade in the hot summer months to families cooling off with a glass of lemonade and mint.

The masonry fountains serve as bird baths for migrating birds that land in the gardens to take a break from their migratory journey and quench their thirst. The feathered visitors rest for a while and offer the human residents an array of songs and whistles before they continue their flyway north for the summer. These lovely traditional homes with their red ceramic tile roofs nestled among pine trees, were being demolished at an alarming rate.

In their place rose a rapidly emerging concrete-and-steel metropolis. Most residents were intoxicated by what they saw as 20th century progress and went on busily and profitably with their daily lives.

Also vanishing during this age of progress was the scent of jasmine in the air carried along by a sea breeze. Old traditional houses and three-story masonry buildings alike had jasmine growing in their courtyards and on their balconies. During spring and summer, pedestrians could walk for blocks with the scent of jasmine keeping them company. But progress replaced that scent with the exhaust fumes of traffic jams, including the new diesel city buses which replaced the old electric tramway railcars that ran on clean, homegrown hydroelectric power.

The golden age of progress also saw a busier and quicker pace of life. Business was booming. Tourism was at an all-time high. And in 1973, a new (26 story) Holiday Inn flagship hotel opened in Beirut. A giant concrete and steel monstrosity that blocked the view of the sea for the old neighborhood on the hill behind it. For centuries, the residents of the old neighborhood had watched the sun set from the balconies of their terraced homes, which collectively resembled an amphitheater overlooking the Mediterranean sea. That view was now blocked by the behemoth reserved for tourists who could afford to pay for a room with a seaside view. So called progress was in full swing.

Lebanon Mountains

Every year, Dimitri spent a good part of summer in the mountains of Lebanon, at Teta's ancestral village, visiting her brother Saleem and his wife, Najla.

From his early childhood, it had been a tradition for Dimitri and Teta to remain in the village for most of the summer while the rest of the family returned to Beirut after the annual summer family reunion.

The mountains of Lebanon are mentioned 71 times in the Bible. They were the refuge of early Christians escaping the oppression and persecution of the Romans. These early Christians, fleeing north, built cave dwellings into the steep cliffs of the mountains, which gave them shelter, safety and protection to practice their faith undisturbed by the persecuting empires that came and went while Teta's ancestors remained. Over time, the cave dwellings were transformed into monasteries by generations of monks skilled as stonemasons. In the centuries that followed, the community grew, and villages began to emerge on the high ground above the valley's cliffs.

One of the oldest monasteries still in service in Lebanon is Deir Mar Antonios. *Deir* means monastery. *Mar* means saint; *Antonios* means Anthony. The monastery is commonly called *Qozaya* in the Aramaic language that Jesus spoke and which the natives still recite in their religious services. *Qozaya* means "the treasure of life" in Jesus's native tongue.

The valley and the cliffs flanking the monastery on both sides are home to the Lebanese Christian Maronites, a sect formed by Saint Maron, who was born in a small town near Antioch in the year 350.

As a young man, Maron ascended the Taurus Mountains, where he felt at home in the quiet solitude of mountain life.

He began as a mystic hermit, camping in the wilderness, praying and fasting. Young Maron studied the native plants for their healing benefits and was said to have healed many ills and wounds of the body as well as those of the soul. He was known for his simplicity and his keen and sensitive ability to discover God's presence in all things.

Maron transitioned from this reclusive life as a hermit to building a community of farmers, masons, carpenters, cooks, bakers and artisans. As the independent and self-sufficient community grew, it attracted attention from the established powers of the time, who began a campaign of persecution.

One of Saint Maron's most capable disciples, Abraham of Cyrrhus (350 to 422 AD), became known as the apostle of Lebanon when he moved the flock into the high mountains of Lebanon. Today, 1600 years later, they remain there, along with their villages, churches and monasteries. The mountain Maronites of Lebanon are much as the earliest travelers found them, not having lost the virtues for which they have long been admired: a welcoming and friendly, yet fierce and resilient people, who have kept their traditions intact for over 1600 years.

Teta and her family loaded up into three cars, and the caravan drove along the coastal highway heading up north. Uncle Victor led the way, with Teta seated in the front passenger seat next to him. Dimitri and his cousins sat in the back, analyzing and debating the football game between Nejmeh and Racing. Samira drove the second car with the newlyweds and their baby, while Uncle George, Aunt Leila, Lina and the younger children completed the caravan.

With Beirut in their rearview mirror, the family approached the neighboring coastal city of Jounieh, an ancient sea fortress situated on a beautiful bay along the Mediterranean Sea, with mountains emerging from the shoreline in a steep grade. Overseeing the bay from 2000 feet above sea level is an iconic 13-ton, majestic bronze statue of Our Lady of Lebanon. She stands with arms outreached in blessing towards Jounieh and Beirut. Residents find comfort and consolation looking up to her.

As the caravan continued along the coast, it entered a tunnel carved into the mountain where it emerged from the sea. At the end of the tunnel, shimmering light appeared on the surface of the Dog River's estuary where it met the Mediterranean Sea. Hundreds of streams and creeks have flowed for millennia from the snow-capped peaks of Mount Lebanon down the ravines and canyons to merge with the Dog River as it makes its way to the coast and into the vast blue sea.

Along the cliffs overlooking the river's estuary lie old stone steps worn and honed down over the centuries by visitors of the historic murals and plaques that have been inscribed into the face of the cliffs. The murals date back millennia, having been built and carved by the ancient stonemasons of the Pharaoh Ramses II, followed by the masons of Assyrian and Babylonian kings, then centuries later by the Greeks and Romans, who were followed by Arab sultans, before the French emperor Napoleon's masons carved his own declaration. The most recent dedication was carved in 1943 to commemorate the independence of Lebanon from France, ushering in this new golden age for the country and its capital city, Beirut.

All the conquering pharaohs, emperors, sultans and kings have come and gone, while Teta's people remained, evolving and absorbing new influences from each epoch-yet remaining faithful to their roots and traditions.

The family stopped to stretch their legs before heading up the centuries-old stone steps to pay homage and read the carvings on the cliff walls. This was a traditional stop they made every summer along the way to Teta's ancestral village.

Climbing back into their cars the family headed up north on the coastal highway. Dimitri gazed out the window at the seemingly endless blue sea, the same unchanged view that his Phoenician ancestors saw and sailed into more than 4000 years ago.

Dimitri's seafaring ancestors had established trading colonies all along the northern coast of the Mediterranean, as far west as the rock of Gibraltar, and along the North African coastline, returning always to their home ports in Phoenicia, today's Lebanon.

Daydreaming as he pondered the sea's expansiveness, Dimitri contemplated the great mystery of the many ancestors that had preceded his presence here today. His family had instilled in him a deeply sentimental connection to the past, creating a strong sense of duty and desire to live a life that would honor those who came before him and propel the great mystery forward into the future. In the daydreams of a 16-year-old, the future held possibilities that were vast, optimistic, hopeful and bright.

As the family continued their journey, they reached the salt producing coastal town of Anfeh. Salt ponds have existed on the rocky shores of Anfeh as far back as the earliest Phoenician records, from 2000 BC. The Phoenicians carved ponds in the seaside rocks, transporting sea water to the salinas. After evaporation by sun and wind, the salt crystals were harvested and traded, by sea and land.

Centuries later, overlooking the rocky shores of Anfeh, European Crusaders built a castle using stones salvaged and taken from Roman ruins. The castle became known as the Monastery of the Watchman (*Deir El Natoor*). It is still inhabited by monks and is supported by the sale of sea salt.

Teta bought two large bags of salt, one for general use and one for pickling turnips and beets, a favorite of her brother Saleem. Then the trip resumed, and the caravan began ascending the foothills of Mount Lebanon along serpentine roads through pine forests, past archaeological sites and various geological formations, surrounded by orchards of olives, grapes, apples and pears, all situated on curving, rustic stone terraces that hugged the contours of the mountains. The villages they passed through shared a similar aesthetic of stone churches, monasteries and traditional Lebanese houses, inhabited by hospitable and friendly villagers.

Ascending to 1200 meters above sea level, the family arrived at the village of Bchaaleh situated on the slope of a mountain and home to old monasteries and traditional stone homes as well as some of the oldest olive trees in the world overlooking the Mediterranean Sea. Among the groves is a protected area designated as a national treasure. A row of olive trees known as the sisters, that are thought to date back over 5000 years and are known as the Olive Trees of Noah. It is said that, after the great flood, a dove delivered an olive branch from the sisters to Noah on the ark, signaling that a time for peace, calm and serenity had arrived. The olive branch continues to be seen as a symbol of a new creation, new expectations and new hope. Over the centuries, the dove and the olive branch have become the universal symbol of peace. Standing among the limbs of these ancient olive trees, visitors from around the world have experienced a spiritual connection while contemplating the thousands of years they have lived through while they have stood there on the mountain.

Not too far from the olive trees are archaeological digs that reveal visible layers of time, each bearing the physical remnants of past civilizations and their many generations of loves, ambitions, triumphs, tragedies, dreams and hopes. While the physical ruins have remained buried for millennia, the spirit of the ancestors continues to live on into the present generation. Walking through the ruins, the imaginative mind can embark on a journey through time.

To the northeast of the village is a citadel built on the ruins of a medieval fortress built atop Phoenician ruins, which were destroyed by the Romans. The story of civilization's evolving and destructive march forward is clearly visible in the layers of stone.

All along the mountainside of Bchaaleh are olive trees growing in the soil between stone terraces. Some are ancient, some centuries old, others decades old, and some are new saplings planted by the villagers, who continue to take pride in their olive-growing heritage. Teta added two kilos of olives and a bottle of olive oil from the local market to her care pack of sweets and savory jars of pickled eggplant (*makdous*) she had saved for Saleem and Najla.

"Teta, tell us stories about your brother Saleem when you two were children," Dimitri asked. He liked hearing the stories Teta told about her brother, even though he'd heard them many times before. With a nostalgic sigh and a smile, Teta described how Saleem always had a special relationship with nature and a way with all living things. "He loved all God's creations, and they all loved him," she recalled. "Bees would land on him, never stinging him. He would welcome them, saying their velvety legs tickled his face." She went on to describe how he used to whistle to the birds and have conversations with them, and how the birds would land on him while singing their songs.

Saleem also had a special affection for trees. "He used to say: 'Even though they are still, they have life and spirit in them.' How he knew it at that young age, I don't know. But he knew, and more importantly, he felt it."

Saleem had a fascination with insects and would observe them closely, making sure to never injure them. All creatures and living things were his friends, she remembered. He would often say: "Even though they look different from us, they see the same sun, breathe the same air and drink the same water as we do. We must be related!"

As Saleem grew older it was not only animals, insects and nature in general that sought his company. People he knew and even strangers felt comfortable confiding in him their concerns and worries, and with him they were also happy to share their good news. Saleem had a way of giving comfort to a troubled soul by offering a sensitive ear. After listening, he would then respond with a poem or short story that addressed the issue and gave great comfort and relief to the listener, who, in Saleem's company, could take a brief break from the suffering, distractions and deafening noise of daily life. Saleem had always lived far removed from the vanities and trappings of the world, while remaining very present to his family, community and work.

Teta looked out into the distance, finding a memory that made her giggle, then said, "Saleem used to give our father fits with some of his questions and ideas. He questioned everything. He used to carve tombstones for our goats and chickens, inscribing words of thanks on the stones for the milk, yogurt, cheese and eggs they provided the family. Our father was embarrassed and told him the neighbors would think we were crazy. Our mother thought it was a great idea and congratulated him on his beautiful stonework. Even though Saleem was our father's stonemason apprentice, his work had more creativity, feeling and soul in it than our father the master mason."

Teta and Saleem's father, Dimitri's great grandfather, Teta continued, "was a conventional, traditional, decent, hard-working and practical man. He saw stone simply as a building block, while his son and apprentice Saleem had an extra sense that was in touch with the earth and saw stone as belonging to the great mystery of creation. He treated each stone with great care and a sense of reverence. He inherited that outlook and sensibility from our mother."

"What about your mother, Teta?" asked Dimitri.

"Your great grandmother Sumaya was the light of the family. A bright, strong, yet modest woman, she carried herself with dignity and a sensitive heart. Being a mountain village midwife, she was respected and loved by all the families in the surrounding villages this side of the mountain, having delivered multiple generations. Even though I was my parents' only daughter, everyone in the village called me 'sister' and Saleem 'brother.' We felt the same way towards them, calling them sister and brother before their names as well. It was your great grandmother Sumaya who encouraged me to go to nursing school in Beirut and earn my degree, which made it possible to start my life in Beirut. She had instilled in her children a solid foundation and a moral compass. It was not only by what she said, but most importantly by her example and the way we saw her carry herself in her daily life.

"After I graduated from nursing school, I decided to stay in Beirut. Even though it was difficult for her to have me far away from her, she carried herself with a brave heart and sensitive soul, telling me, I have taught you all I can, my dear child, and tried my best to orient you along a solid and sound path." Teta then quoted a sage from her village who migrated to America in the 19th century before she was born. Khalil Gibran once wrote:

Your children are not your children.
They are the sons and daughters of Life's longing for
    itself.
They come through you but not from you,
And though they are with you yet they belong not to you.
You may give them your love but not your thoughts,
For they have their own thoughts.
You may house their bodies but not their souls,
For their souls dwell in the house of tomorrow.
You may strive to be like them,
But seek not to make them like you.
For life goes not backward nor tarries with yesterday.
You are the bows from which your children as living
    arrows are sent forth.
The archer sees the mark upon the path of the infinite,

And he bends you with his might that his arrows may go
    swift and far.
Let your bending in the archer's hand be for gladness,
For even as he loves the arrow that flies,
So he also loves the bow that is stable.

"I wish I had been able to meet her," said Dimitri.

"I wish you did, my dear. You would have loved her. I feel she is looking over us all, today and always."

As the cars made their way towards the Kadisha Valley, known as the "valley of the saints," Sunday church bells near and far rang, raising a collective and festive echo throughout the valley on a beautiful summer day in Mount Lebanon.

After church let out, youth and kids would gather at the church bell tower and take turns ringing the bells in a joyful competition, with each having a turn at trying to pull the rope while reaching new heights. As the heavy steel bell swung, its momentum would pull the rope higher, sending the kids upward and making them momentarily airborne while the bell's clang echoed through the valley.

Teta was happy and full of joy as she started spotting various landmarks of trees, homes, terraces and orchards that she recognized as leading to Saleem and Najla's home.

Saleem's house was an old traditional Lebanese stone house, one he had built with his father next to his grandparents' house, about a hundred meters up the hill from his great grandparents' house. The whole area below, along the rim of the valley, had stone houses dating back to generations of Saleem and Teta's ancestors. Each generation of stonemasons built a traditional home, married, started a family and worked their trade, building and maintaining stone monasteries, churches, schools and clinics, as well as the more than 3000 stone hermitages in the valley below.

As the car made a long, arcing turn along the rim of the valley, Saleem's apple orchards appeared to open their branches to welcome them. Then, a little farther up the hill, Teta's old house, the one she was born and raised in, came into view, nestled among the trees and framed by stone terraces.

When the caravan made its way into the driveway, the first to greet them was Saleem and Najla's old dog Natoor. No sooner had his first welcoming barks sounded than the whole extended family and friends began spilling out of the house, offering animated welcomes full of warm hugs and kisses from aunts, uncles, cousins and lifetime friends.

"*Ahlan! Ahlan wa sahlan*!" they repeated over and over with each new wave of hugs and kisses.

Finally, everyone settled down with a glass of lemonade and began to catch up on family news while the cousins played outside with the goats and chickens, weaving through the apple and pear orchards.

Teta's brother Saleem had remained in the village all his life, while his siblings went to the big city to seek their future, careers, fortunes, notoriety and all the things that city people seek and do. Saleem carried on the family tradition, becoming a master stonemason like his father, grandfather and great grandfather before him. He married his school sweetheart, Najla, and they raised their family in the mountains.

Dimitri had loved spending time with Saleem every summer since he was a little boy, fiddling with tools by Saleem's side. At age 10 he started learning and working the trade in earnest and had now been Saleem's official stonemason apprentice for the past six summers, as the two worked on building a stone cabin together.

At 76, Saleem was ostensibly retired from the trade but did not feel quite himself unless he worked some stone as part of his daily routine. He had spent over half a century with his hammer and chisels working most every day, except on Sundays. The old stonemason still worked corner stones to keep his angles and edges sharp, plumb and level. He also carved keystones with religious and nature themes of vines and flowers to keep his craft and creativity in practice.

Saleem looked forward to Dimitri's stay each summer, happy to be passing along his masonry skills to a new generation at a time when young people interested in those skills were becoming rare. Saleem's own son, Najeeb, had left the village as a young man and moved to the coastal city of Tripoli, where he established a successful import-export office near the port.

"Imagine!" Saleem would say to Dimitri, shaking his head. "He makes a living sitting behind a desk talking on the telephone all day. What kind of work is that?" Dimitri sensed that Saleem wished that Najeeb had followed in his footsteps, carrying on the family tradition. He could tell the old man missed his son.

Saleem would then nod his head with acceptance, saying, "Everyone is different and should be free to follow their dream. Najeeb likes what he is doing, and he is good at it. He has the gift of communication and the social skills of making connections. He also has a track record of being trustworthy and respected for his ability to plan thoroughly, execute and deliver." And with that, Saleem's face revealed joy and even pride.

However, the old stonemason still believed and lived by the traditional code of "*Min arak jabeenak Ta'kul Khibzak.*" (From the sweat of your brow, you eat your bread.) Anything else seemed to him opportunistic, dishonorable, … or at least questionable.

This code of honest labor was how his ancestors had survived through centuries fraught with political upheaval and hardship brought on by occupying empires that had come and gone while the villages of Mount Lebanon remained self-sufficient and its people fiercely independent. Every family in the village contributed their surplus harvest to the church, which then distributed food among the poorer villagers, ensuring that everyone had what they needed to survive, especially during the harsh winter months of cold weather and deep snow.

On the first day of work in the field, Saleem and Dimitri headed to the far side of the apple orchard to work on the stone terrace being prepared for next year's planting of the apple saplings Najla had been cultivating. Dimitri, as young people often do, was happy to show the old man how strong and capable he had become by enthusiastically collecting field stones and placing them in rows from which to pick. Dimitri pulled up the random field stones by digging out the edges with a pickaxe, then squatting down and deadlifting them from the earth. After a couple of hours, a few dozen rocks lay in groups, like pieces of a puzzle.

In building a dry-stack terrace with random rubble, it takes a good eye to visualize how the stones can work together to form an interlocking solid and sound whole. Saleem would direct Dimitri on which stone to pick next, and it would invariably fit solidly into place. The years of experience made it look easy, and Dimitri began to see the stone's unique shape and its potential placing as he hit his stride and got into the flow of stacking the stones in a tight pattern. After a section was built, the master mason and his apprentice would step back, with both heads nodding in approval, before quenching their thirst using a ceramic *briq*, filled by the fresh stream nearby.

Occasionally Dimitri, as young men often do, would get caught up in a competition with himself and hastily move on to another stone while leaving a potential weak link in his work. Saleem would point it out, saying, "Remember, building a stone wall is like building a sound life. It's important not to force things, but rather with patience and clarity know what to look for." He would then pick a stone that had a slightly different angle, and it would fit perfectly with the one next to it. "There." He would add. "They were meant to be with each other." Like a Cupid of stones, Saleem would say, "See how they complement each other. They will live happily next to each other, with neither one putting an uneven pressure on the other or leaving a weak connection that over time could unravel them from each other, affecting the rest of the wall. The stone wall is like a family. Each stone is different in shape and size, but put together they make a complete, solid and sound whole."

Dimitri enjoyed learning and working with Saleem.

His great uncle was a man of contrasts: pious and modest in his most inner being, yet outwardly lively and engaging in a traditional Lebanese way. He was loyal to his family, community and church, while open and welcoming to all. Though he remained all his life in the village of his birth, his love of reading created a deep interest in other cultures and religions. While intrigued and amused by the differences, he found joy in seeing the commonality of humanity. "So many ancient civilizations and distant lands with different races, cultures, traditions and religions, but at the core we are all the same," he would often say. "We want a good life for our children, families and communities."

Saleem loved to read. He had an open mind and heart. "While I have lived all my life in the mountains, I have traveled and visited the world through books and learned a lot by observing nature around me, which taught me how things work and relate to each other," he once told Dimitri.

At night after supper, Saleem would smoke his pipe, sitting in his chair with his old trusty dog Natoor curled up next to him. He would gaze up into the heavens and contemplate the great mystery with a thankful heart and a prayer. He was grounded, yet expansive, like an ancient cedar tree deeply rooted in the earth it germinated from, yet with branches extending out and embracing the universe.

Walking together in town, Dimitri noticed how Saleem was generous with his time and attention to others, and how he gave freely of his spirit. People liked being around him and felt safe and uplifted by his presence, even if it was just in passing with a simple traditional exchange of *"Sabah el kheir"* (morning of goodness) and the response of *"Sabah el nour"* (morning of light).

Since Dimitri's father died, Saleem had made it his mission every summer to teach Dimitri the timeless basics of navigating what he called "a sound life." His tenets were few and simple but applied to all things ventured. At the core they were, first and foremost: love, respect of self and of others, truth, dedication, and courage.

Dimitri always welcomed the opportunity to show Saleem what he had learned, and Saleem was always encouraging and congratulating Dimitri when he saw him practice these basic tenets in various aspects of his life.

Every summer, while working with Saleem, Dimitri experienced physical, mental and spiritual growth. It thrilled Teta to see her grandson working and learning from the family sage.

The two spent most of each day working together. Saleem missed not having his son to work with, and Dimitri missed not having a father. They would spend the first part of the day working on stone, while the afternoon was dedicated to nurturing and cultivating the orchard's trees and vines. Natoor kept them company everywhere they went. Like Saleem, the dog had passed his prime, but he still took pride in being the guardian of the chickens, goats and his human family. In his old age, not much could get Natoor worked up. The old dog had seen it all, from encounters with wild striped hyenas and jackals to wildcats and foxes. Natoor's confident and mellow disposition remained very much in touch with his surroundings and its familiar smells, along with its sounds and natural rhythms and cycles. If he detected something unusual, he would get up from his resting spot and confidently saunter forth to investigate.

He still had an imposing bark and a full set of teeth and had enough in him to give chase to his nemesis, the fox. The chase in years past had covered half the mountainside in a match of cunning, sheer will and determination. Now it had become limited to a 30-meter sprint by Natoor, just enough of a bluff to scare off the fox. The fox had also aged past his prime and felt relieved he didn't have to run for kilometers on end, either. Natoor and the fox, while adversaries, were in a way fond of each other, and their encounters fulfilled a basic instinct. After the short sprint, both had a little bounce in their step and momentarily looked as if they were still in their prime.

Before sunset, Saleem would make his ritual rounds with Natoor and Dimitri, securing the chickens and goats in the barn for the night. But not before leaving the fox some remnants from the dinner table. With a puzzled look, Dimitri once asked, "Why are you leaving the fox food? I thought you wanted to keep him away from the chickens!" Saleem explained that the fox had become part of life for him and Natoor and recalled how he had known this fox since he was a little pup, having seen him go through the cycles of life. First as a survivor, then for a long span of time a mature, robust hunter, before entering his senior years of decline.

"Lately, like Natoor and me, he has slowed down considerably, which for a hunter could be fatal, especially in winter when the snow blankets the earth and food is scarce. So, by leaving him some food on that rock over there, he knows there will be something for him at night if he wasn't successful during the day."

The sun had started to set as Saleem and Dimitri made their way along the stone pathway leading to the house. As they got closer, they could see Teta and Najla through the living room window, illuminated by the lamp's warm yellow light. They were both working on their cross-stitch, a traditional art form they had learned from their mothers when they were little girls, over 70 years ago. Teta still cross-stitched often, even in Beirut. It had long been her evening quiet, meditative time. Over the years, she had produced many beautiful pieces that became gifts to her family, friends and church. This summer she had been working on a piece featuring the Lord's prayer for her grandson Dimitri.

The old stonemason and his apprentice entered the house, greeting Teta and Najla and complimenting them on their beautiful work. Dimitri washed up and wished everyone a good night: *"Tusbaho ala kheir."* They responded: *"Tusbah ala kheir ya habibi."* Dimitri asked Saleem if he could borrow a book to read from the family bookcase.

"Of course, take your pick. Just remember to return it to where you found it when you are done."

Dimitri, mindful of Teta's poetic quote on the way to the mountains, chose a book by Khalil Gibran, the local poet and artist who migrated to America in 1895. Gibran's poetry had been well received internationally. His seminal book *The Prophet*, composed of 28 poetic essays, had been translated to more than 100 languages. Saleem and Teta often quoted passages from it. Dimitri gently pulled the book off the shelf and walked to the hallway, petting Natoor's head and jowls before turning and heading to his room. Natoor lingered at the start of the hallway, wagging his tail, until Dimitri entered his room and closed the door behind him. At that point, Natoor turned around and went to curl up on the rug next to Teta and Najla.

Dimitri lay down on his bed with the feeling of deep contentment that comes from a day of honest and productive labor and a body replenished with healthy, natural food, in a house filled with love. Dimitri opened Gibran's book and read a passage on the spiritual aspect of work.

> You work that you may keep pace with the earth and the
>   soul of the earth.
> For to be idle is to become a stranger unto the seasons,
>   and to step out of life's procession, that marches in
>   majesty and proud submission towards the infinite.
> To love life through labor is to be intimate with life's
>   inmost secret.
> All knowledge is vain save when there is work, and all
>   work is empty save when there is love;
> And when you work with love you bind yourself to
>   yourself, and to one another, and to God.
> And what is it to work with love?
> It is to weave the cloth with threads drawn from your
>   heart, even as if your beloved were to wear that
>   cloth.
> It is to build a house with affection, even as if your
>   beloved were to dwell in that house.
> It is to sow seeds with tenderness and reap the harvest
>   with joy, even as if your beloved were to eat the fruit.
> It is to charge all things you fashion with a breath of your

own spirit.

Work is love made visible.

*   *   *

Dimitri put the book down on the table beside him and visualized the work he and Saleem did on the stone cabin earlier, while listening to the rhythmic soundwaves of the summer cicadas. A gentle breeze made its way through the window into his room, carrying the scent of the pine and cedar woods it had passed through on this beautiful, starlit summer night in Mount Lebanon.

Saleem headed to the kitchen to brew chamomile tea for Teta and Najla, who continued creating art with needle and thread. After a while he emerged from the kitchen with three ceramic cups of his herbal brew and set them on the table in front of the women while congratulating them both on their beautiful work. As the three sat sipping their tea and reminiscing about good friends who had passed away, Saleem shifted the conversation to the present. *"Shu akhbar Beirut?"* he asked. "What's the news in Beirut?"

"Tense!" answered Teta. "There is a lot going on behind the scenes. Everything seems fine on the surface. Planes come and planes go. Ships come and ships go. Business is booming, but it's all *ala kaf afreet.*" (It's all in the palm of the devil. An old expression that means things are precarious and could go wrong at any time when the *afreet* decides to clasp its hand.) She went on to explain that there had been a rise in street skirmishes and clashes between the PLO and the Lebanese Christian Nationalists.

"Dimitri hasn't been the same this year," Teta said with a worried expression. "He's becoming aware of politics and attending meetings with his older cousin Jabril, who he loves and looks up to as an older brother. Dimitri is a good boy and helps the family a lot. But he doesn't listen to Samira or me anymore when it comes to politics and the groups that he has increasingly become involved with. I wish he had his father around. Sometimes I wonder if these groups are a substitute for that absence."

*   *   *

While Dimitri loved playing and joking with his friends and cousins, in private he had a stoic and somber side. Having experienced loss at an early age made him more serious than other kids his age. He was also at a point in his life where he was looking to break out and forge his own identity by becoming part of something he saw as meaningful and important.

Teta, with a worried voice, turned to her brother and said, "I hope you can talk to him and see what's going on. I know he loves you and respects your outlook and opinions. You're about the only one he seriously listens to anymore."

Saleem nodded silently, acknowledging his sister's concern. "Don't worry, I'll talk with him when the time is right," he said calmly and confidently. "Dimitri will be okay. It could be a phase he is going through." Teta smiled, feeling reassured. Najla was reassuring as well, and the three returned to sipping tea and sharing nostalgic memories.

The next morning at dawn, Dimitri woke up to the rooster's crow announcing the start of a new day. Not long after, the mourning doves began cooing as they basked in the sun's first rays, followed by the chirping and tweeting of birds in the tree outside his bedroom window. The natural concert built to a crescendo of rejoicing at the rising sun.

Dimitri got up, made his bed, and headed to the basin of water, cupping his hands and filling them with the source of life. He splashed water on his face and repeated it two more times. Teta had taught him what had become his morning ritual from the early days of preparing for school. Splash the source of life on your face three times, she advised, and start your day with clarity, "*Ya Ayook*" (You bright one).

As Dimitri opened the door to the hallway leading to the kitchen, he was greeted with the aroma of thyme, sesame seeds and fresh bread. Teta and Najla were up early and had fired up the *saj*, a large, steel half-dome with a fire source beneath it. They were cooking *manouche*, the Lebanese traditional breakfast bread smothered with thyme, sesame seeds and olive oil with optional toppings of mint, goat cheese and tomato. On days of heavy lifting, eggs fried in olive oil and topped with goat cheese and sumac would be added, for a sturdy country breakfast that's suitable for serious labor.

Dimitri entered the kitchen, greeting Teta and Najla with "*Sabah el kheir*" (morning of goodness). They responded with "*Sabah el nour*" (morning of light). Dimitri noticed that Teta had a peacefully contented smile, a certain look she had when she was in the mountains.

While Teta was always positive, warm and affectionate, in Beirut she was also often serious, worried and under pressure, watching over the extended family's welfare while volunteering at clinics in a busy city environment.

Here in the mountains, the pressure was off. It's where her spirit and soul belonged and where she felt at peace.

After graduating from nursing school in Beirut, she had gone to work at the American University Hospital. Then she married and had three children: Samira and Dimitri's two uncles, Gabriel and Victor.

Teta continued to be the pillar of strength for her extended family, through good times and bad, always with an unwavering spirit of self-lessness and dedication. What she thought of as her family went beyond blood relatives and transcended boundaries of nationality, race, class and sect. In her later years, she continued to volunteer, providing medical mentorship to a new generation of nurses and medical workers who were helping to take care of the poor, orphans and refugees.

Teta was a devout Christian in the truest sense of the word; she never overtly displayed her religion and was never opinionated or preachy about it. She wore her cross on a chain underneath her shirt. It was not a fashion statement or display, but rather a private and personal devotion that was only visible to others through the actions and work she did in her daily life.

Over half a century ago, as an inspired, young, educated, ambitious and spirited woman, Teta found Beirut's tempo in line with her highly energetic sense of purpose and responsibility to humanity. She loved the city and its people. But here in the mountains, in her ancestral village, she felt like the innocent child she had been long ago, before becoming a young woman fully aware of the many neglected needs of humanity and dedicating her life to doing something about it.

"Come sit down and eat your breakfast," Teta said. "Saleem already ate. He's out with Natoor, feeding the chickens and goats." Dimitri rolled a manouche with goat cheese and mint.

"I'm so happy to be here again, Teta. I can't wait to work on the stone cabin maalem Saleem and I started building five summers ago."

"He's very happy to have you here as well. It gives him purpose," Teta said. "Now finish your breakfast so you can have strength and energy for your work."

From a distance came the sound of paws tapping the floor. Natoor made a straight line to Dimitri with his tail wagging and drumming against the kitchen table and chairs. Dimitri greeted him with equal enthusiasm and affection.

Teta tried to contain her laughter, but then sternly called out *"Yalla barra!"* reminding Natoor he was not allowed in the kitchen. He headed out to the porch where he could see the chickens and goats, still wagging his tail. Natoor knew Teta was serious and strict, but he also knew that she was sweet and loving.

"Sabaah el kheir!" announced Saleem as he entered the kitchen. *"Sabaah el noor ya maalem Saleem!"* answered Dimitri.

"Are you ready to work on the cabin?"

"Ready!"

The two headed out to Saleem's workshop down the hill on a pathway leading to a flat patch of land overlooking the valley. The workshop had been built of stone and timber by Saleem's grandfather. It housed sets of pulleys, levers, wheelbarrows, jacks, hammers, chisels, trowels and levels of all sizes, from a small hand-sized wooden spirit level with a glass cylinder and bubble to long clear flexible plastic tubing used to find the level between long spans.

In the old days, the tubing was made of goat and sheep intestines. Goats' intestines stretched around 30 meters in length, while those of sheep were around 40. The tubing was filled with water and allowed to hang between two points of a structure. When the water line on the opposing ends of the tube became still, the two points were level with each other.

The workspace outside the shop was an open-sky courtyard with numerous stacks of stone in various parts of the yard. Situated underneath the shaded canopy of a large baloot oak tree were three heavy-duty workbenches. On them lay stones at various stages of completion. Some were roughly shaped building blocks, others intricately carved works of art.

Dimitri worked independently on his own bench, next to the master mason. Saleem sang spiritual songs while the two hammered in unison with a rhythmic and meditative tempo, shaping and finishing the building blocks for the cabin. Dimitri whistled along through the parts of the songs he didn't have memorized … and Dimitri whistled a lot.

It was a concert that attracted a variety of wildlife. Birds would land on the baloot tree's branches, listening curiously to the whistles and songs, while shimaisi lizards sunned themselves on the stone stacks, intrigued by the vibration of the hammer and chisel. Meanwhile the goats grazed close by, under the watchful eye of Natoor.

This was to be Saleem's last structural build of a long career as a master stonemason. His love of the trade was eternal, and he felt grateful to be able to pass on his knowledge, but his bones and joints were getting too old for the physical requirements.

"Now that you are retired, why don't you come and visit Beirut? It would be nice to see you more often," Dimitri said. Saleem apologetically and earnestly answered, "I would love to see you and the family more, *ya habibi*. But the city is not for me. I belong in the mountains. There is too much noise in the city for my spirit, which only understands itself in the serenity of the mountains and the meditative work of stonemasonry."

This resonated with Dimitri. He, too, felt his best in the mountains. His best self physically, mentally and spiritually. But he had grown up in Beirut and come of age amid the excitement and expansiveness of a capital city with an international air and seaport, a city that looked out into the expansiveness of the world while welcoming influences from all over the globe.

"Someday I would like to live in the mountains," he said. Saleem smiled.

"I would love that. You are already a fine mason and can work with George, Emile, Charbel, Maron and my other brothers at the fraternity of church and monastery builders. But first, finish your education. You should always know that you have a home here. This stone cabin we have been building together is for you. You have earned it with your sweat, effort and good company. In the future, when you marry and raise a family, you can add to it, as I did with the stone cabin I built when I was an apprentice over sixty years ago."

Dimitri with profound thanks to Saleem, reflected on his gratitude for summers he spent in the mountains. He had built inner strength and the kind of confidence that comes from knowing that your base is sound and that your people love you. No amount of money or position in life in the future can ever replace that.

The old stonemason and his apprentice took a water break, drinking from a ceramic *briq* filled with ice-cold water from the stream nearby. During the break, Saleem broached the subject that had his sister worried. "Teta tells me you are interested in politics now, and that there are a lot of political rumblings in Beirut. What have you found? What is going on?"

Dimitri sighed heavily, like someone who had just set down a heavy load. "Well, *ya maalem* Saleem, there have been many meetings and speakers at school clubs and at private homes. I went to some with my friends, and it's sometimes confusing. They all have good ideas about helping the country and each other in a spirit of camaraderie and brotherhood that makes me happy to be part of the meetings. But then there is also talk of the dark clouds of war rolling in, and the things we should be prepared for and prepared to do."

Dimitri went on to describe how recent meetings had become less about optimistic visions of progress and more about heated speeches laden with nationalism, patriotism and the imminent dangers the country and the constitution was facing, while opposing groups talked about their grievances, just causes, and bringing down the government.

"After our meetings, it's become common to have trouble with clashes on the street. Our group leader was stopped at a checkpoint at Tel al-Zaatar and questioned for six hours before being released. Now he wants us all to wear sidearms. It's getting quite tense in certain parts of the city."

Saleem listened with lips tight, eyebrows lifted and his head alternately nodding in understanding and pivoting side to side disapprovingly.

"I hope the politicians can still find a peaceful way to resolve the impasse. It's hard to do when emotions are whipped up at an all-time high. That's when human beings tend to create problems for themselves and others."

After a pause, Saleem went on to explain how civilization has had a bad record when it comes to war, and how war has not diminished with the rise of civilization or democracy. "In the last 3421 years of recorded civilization, only 268 years have seen no war. It's not a good record."

Then, more hopefully, he added, "May our Lady of Lebanon lead us to a different way and a brighter future of peace. It's the universal desire of humanity to achieve peace, yet it has been so elusive. Since the beginning of time, the ideal social and political condition for humanity to achieve happiness is peace. Peace is present when the life of a community is not disturbed by attempts of individuals and their factions to pursue selfish, expansive and controlling ambitions, while turning against other groups to realize them. I hope the politicians find a solution soon. No one wins in wars. Even the winners lose. Those who survive, like my late uncle Boutros, who returned home after the First World War lost something inside them that is true, innocent and bright. Stay clear-headed, aware, optimistic and brave, Dimitri. Beware of false counsel, my dear. There is a lot of it leading to war."

Dimitri felt concerned yet relieved that there was an explanation for all the false actions taking place in the city the past year.

Saleem, putting on a contemplative smile, added, "Maybe our brothers and sisters the Quakers have the right idea, but unfortunately that's not part of our history and tradition in this volatile part of the world. Peace should always be sought after. But sometimes things deteriorate to a point where you are left with limited choices, and you must defend yourself. The only legitimate and honorable war is one of defense, not one of aggression, conquest, theft and expansiveness. *Inshalla Kheir wa salaam!"* (God willing, goodness and peace!)

"Keep in mind that ultimately the only real victory and triumph is internal and personal. It is the enlightenment of the mind and the improvement of one's own character."

Dimitri took in the simplicity of that last statement in silence. It resonated with his inner being and became a bright and clear beacon, whose light cut through the darkness and the political smoke and mirrors that were leading to the many wrong actions taking place in Beirut.

"Enlightenment of the mind and improvement of character," Dimitri repeated.

Saleem smiled gently at Dimitri, recognizing that an important, simple and true lifetime point of reference had been imparted and that it had been understood and appreciated by his apprentice.

The two returned to work, with Saleem singing spiritual songs of peace and Dimitri whistling in unison while the hammers striking the chisels of both masons rang through the valley.

The stonemason works in stone and finds the shape of his own soul in it. The things he builds and leaves for many generations to come are a testament to his love, hope and faith in humanity. The dwellings he builds are meant to last for centuries, and even Millenia, with the intention of offering shelter, safety and happiness to people he will never meet. Generations will dwell in his creations long after he departs his earthly life and will create their own lives and memories in the dwellings, churches and monasteries he helped build.

The day had come for the keystone to be carved before placing it at the apex of the arch, locking and stabilizing the curving blocks of the left and right sides and holding them all together. On this special stone, Saleem took a lead pencil and wrote in Arabic *Dar Al Salaam* (House of Peace) for Dimitri to carve into the stone.

Saleem was a fine calligrapher who would often put ink to paper in the evenings after supper while his wife, Najla, worked on her cross-stitch. It was the old couple's nightly ritual of being together while working on their own meditative and creative projects.

Before the work began on the keystone, Dimitri practiced and honed the carving skills Saleem had taught him. Then, placing his hammer and chisels next to the keystone, he walked down to the nearby spring and cupped his hands together, gathering the source of life in his palms before splashing it on his face three times, then running his wet hands and fingers through his hair. He felt refreshed and ready for the task ahead.

As Dimitri headed back to his workbench, Saleem exclaimed in an operatic voice: "*Ah, ya ayook!*" (Ah, you bright one!) The two laughed, remembering that Teta had often called him that since he was a little boy. Dimitri then settled into a focused state of mind before picking up his tools and beginning the task of carving the words into the keystone. Great care and finesse were given to the placement and angle of the chisel before gentle, yet decisive taps brought the letters into relief, setting them in stone.

When the work was complete, Dimitri and Saleem stood the stone up and stepped back to view it. "Beautiful! masterfully done!" said Saleem. It was a crowning moment after years of hard work the two had put into the stone cabin and the many conversations they'd had along the way as Dimitri was coming of age.

"We are going to miss you when you leave, Dimitri," Saleem said. "Take care of your Teta, mother, aunts and cousins in Beirut."

Dimitri's heart was filled with love and charged with confidence. "Don't you worry, *ya maalem* Saleem. I'm a man now, and I'm on duty." The old stonemason chuckled internally at the notion of a 16-year-old being a man, yet he admired Dimitri's earnestness and sense of familial responsibility. With a joyful heart and a solemn expression befitting the occasion, he simply responded: "Bravo, Dimitri! I am proud of you."

The next morning after breakfast, Uncle Boulus and Dimitri's cousin Jabril came by for a manouche breakfast with goat cheese and mint and a cup of tea and honey before picking up Dimitri to go to Boy Scout camp.

Summer camp

Every summer since they were little boys, Dimitri and Jabril had spent the last two weeks of the summer in the mountains at camp, where they would reunite with their Scout friends, many of whom they hadn't seen since the summer before.

The first day of camp was always a festive reunion among old friends, recounting stories of camps past and looking forward to what was ahead. The camp provided a mixture of learning activities: Bible study, civic duty studies, first aid, survival skills, self-defense, marksmanship and a variety of games and sports.

After a full day of learning, practicing and training, the Scouts would share a hearty dinner of goat stew, potatoes and green beans over rice while they gathered around the campfire sharing stories, some comical, some entertaining and others inspirational. The bond of friendship grew stronger every year in these weeks, just as another growth ring develops around a cedar tree with each passing year.

*　　*　　*

At 9 p.m., it was time to put out the fire, and at 9:30 it was lights-out and quiet. After everyone had settled in their tents, Dimitri headed up the hill past a large rock outcropping and leaned back into the trunk and roots of a large ancient cedar. Covering himself with his sleeping bag, he looked up and gazed into the heavens filled with countless clusters of stars extending into infinity. All was quiet, except for the occasional gentle breeze making its way through the cedars' branches and carrying its scent into the surrounding air on a beautiful summer night in the mountains of Lebanon.

With the dawn of a new day, the sun began to rise behind Mount Lebanon, and the light filtered through the cedar branches, a vision that would stay with Dimitri all his life. His meditative state of mind transitioned to a prayer of gratitude before it was harshly interrupted by the sound of the bugle calling everyone to fall in line for morning roll call, followed by the national anthem.

This year's camp felt different than camps of years past. There were daily speeches given by adults that the Scouts had never seen before. They were nationalistic speeches laden with patriotism and the need to protect the country. The speeches were given with conviction and a sense of urgency.

Another difference this year was the marksmanship training. The air rifles of years past were replaced with rifles that used live ammunition: .22 for the kids and 223 & 308 for the older teenagers. Another change was that the round paper bull's-eyes of years past had been replaced by a silhouette of a human figure. To the teenage boys, it was an exciting upgrade and seemingly all fun and games.

Another new unusual activity was a daily race to fill and stack sandbags to form a wall one meter high by two meters wide. At the sound of the whistle, the Scouts scrambled to pick up shovels. Dimitri walked over and picked up his shovel by gripping the metal neck of the spade and using it as a mason uses a trowel. Steadily and methodically, he began shoveling sand into burlap bags and establishing a rhythm that had him complete his wall of neatly interlocking sandbags long before his fellow scouts did. Not one for remaining idle, he continued to fill sandbags and hand them over to his friends.

Teta always said the Lord had made Dimitri's hands strong, like those of his great grandfather Boulus. It enabled him to create, build, plant and cultivate as his ancestors did. He came, after all, from strong masonry and farming stock. In stark contrast to his physical strength, there was a modesty, vulnerability and gentleness about him. And while he was a typical teenager in many ways, joking and playing with his friends, he also had a private, stoic and sensitive side to him. Often, he enjoyed being by himself while contemplating and taking pictures of nature with his Kodak Brownie camera.

The past six years as Saleem's apprentice had developed both internal and external strength in him. His hands were calloused from handling a heavy hammer and working with stone all summer. In Beirut, he worked after school at his uncle's neighborhood grocery store as a delivery boy, gripping propane tanks and climbing up flights of stairs to deliver them to customers.

His hands looked like eagle's talons, but with fingertips that had a high degree of tactile sensitivity, enabling him to manipulate the most complex of rope knots. His arms, especially his right hammering arm, had biceps and forearms with veins running across them, that resembled a road map.

By now, he was able to crack a walnut shell with his bare hands: a small feat he performed around the campfire at night, to the delight of his friends and the amazement of the older captains in their twenties who, try as they might, could not crack the shell. That is, except for Yuhanna, a blacksmith from the neighboring village. After dinner, the Scouts sat around the campfire nibbling on walnuts and sharing memorable stories, with an abundance of laughter and camaraderie, under a beautiful summer sky filled with countless clusters of stars that seemed so close and clear up in the mountains, far from the city lights.

In the summer of 1974, however, the campfire atmosphere was dampened by dark stories of the troubles in Beirut and the street skirmishes and clashes taking place between the Lebanese Christian Nationalists and the PLO. The stories reinforced the political speeches the Scouts heard every day.

The Nationalist cause of defending the country and its constitution began to be understood intellectually and, more importantly, emotionally, as the brotherhood and camaraderie formed a solid bond among the Scouts, who were united and committed to a cause they swore to uphold. The indoctrination was complete.

*　　*　　*

The last day of camp was filled with sad goodbyes. The Scouts knew they might not see each other until next summer, but they had no idea how different the summer of 1975 would be.

The neighborhood

Heading back to Beirut from the mountains was always bittersweet for Dimitri. He loved the mountains and already missed Saleem, Najla and Natoor. But he was also excited to be returning to Beirut and catching up with the neighborhood friends he had grown up with.

When the family returned to their building, Dimitri brought the suitcases up to the apartment. Teta began unpacking and asked Dimitri to head out to the neighborhood stores to buy a short list of groceries. The dutiful grandson headed down the stairs, skipping four steps at a time before landing in the lobby and heading out into the concrete and steel metropolis of Beirut.

He crossed the street to the neighborhood barbershop owned by his friend's grandfather, Khawaja Joseph. The street outside the barbershop was filled with noise and chaos: cars, horns, gasoline fumes, jackhammers being used to fix a broken water main, mobile vendors calling out their merchandise, and people scurrying about their daily business.

Those who entered Khawaja Joseph's barbershop would immediately sense that they had entered a very different environment, a place of decorum and order. Men in crisp white shirts, black suits and neckties sat in leather chairs, and above them on the wall was a large portrait of Pierre Gemayel, set within a fine white linen matte and a formal lacquered black frame. It's a portrait of a clean-shaven, well-groomed gentleman looking upward and into the future with the intense gaze of a hawk.

Pierre Gemayel had been, in his youth, the captain of the Lebanese national football team. He was also Lebanon's first international referee. Educated at Saint Joseph University, he studied pharmacy at the French faculty of medicine in Beirut and opened a successful pharmacy downtown. He married his lifetime sweetheart, Genevieve, a dynamic trailblazer in her own right. She was a pilot and artist fluent in three languages. The couple had six children.

When Pierre Gemayel entered political life, he became an influential member of parliament as the founder of the Nationalist Kataeb Phalange Party, which was committed to a Western-oriented Lebanon. Sheik Pierre, the family man and godfather to countless families, ran things from the mountainous Matn area all the way down through east Beirut into the city port that was the lifeblood of the country.

*　　*　　*

The owner of the barbershop, Khawaja Joseph, was an old friend of Pierre Gemayel and a member of his political party. Khawaja Joseph ran a tight ship. Everything in the shop was orderly and in tip-top shape. All the implements and tools of the trade were kept in fine working order, disinfected and sterilized after each customer and then lined up precisely the same way at each station.

The fragrance of Pinaud talcum powder and aftershave filled the air. Smoking was not permitted. To be a barber at Khawaja Joseph's shop required maintaining a high standard. His four barbers had been with him for many years. The most senior had been there for over three decades; the most recent to join the team did so seven years ago, when another barber named George passed away and his seat remained vacant for a year.

As a young man, Joseph studied at the seminary with the intention of becoming a priest. As life turned out, he became a barber instead after having practiced his skill on the heads of many monks. Joseph moved to the city, started his business, married, and with his wife, Marie, raised a family in the building above his shop.

Not all the men sitting in the barbershop were there to get a haircut or a shave. It was also a gathering place where the *Closed* sign would be placed at the door to allow meetings to take place in the back, with discussions about politics and current events. It was a place where people made connections, struck deals and solved disputes, with Khawaja Joseph as a trusted and fair mediator.

Once a week, three large black sedans would pull up to the barbershop. Men in black suits, ties and starched white shirts would step out of the cars onto the sidewalk; before Pierre Gemayel would calmly emerge and head into the barbershop under the watchful eyes of his bodyguards and the admiring glances of the neighbors.

The barbershop had a close-knit yet austere atmosphere. Aside from the organized private meetings, it was eerily quiet. Words were kept to a minimum, sharing decibel space with the sound of folding newspaper pages, the crisp clicks of scissors and the back-and-forth rhythmic sound of a straight razor being stropped on leather.

The grandfather clock's pendulum swung precisely in a rhythmic tick-tock while the ceiling fans rotated smoothly, whisper-quiet as they produced a cooling breeze on a hot summer day.

Unlike the busy and boisterous coffee shop down the street, the barbershop was where people came to calm down and enter a meditative atmosphere while getting a haircut or a straight-razor shave before an important meeting, job interview, birthday, baptism, wedding or funeral. Whatever the occasion, one thing was certain; a man left the place feeling better than when he entered it.

When Dimitri stepped into the barbershop, Khawaja Joseph let out a warm, welcoming greeting. *"Ahlan! Ahlan!* Dimitri, how were the mountains?"

"They were great, but it's also good to be back in the neighborhood. How is Elie?"

"He's looking forward to your return. He's probably on the football field with his friends."

"I'm headed to the field after I get Teta some groceries."

"Welcome back home. Say hello to the family and come in for a haircut, you're starting to look like a *khanfoos.* Both laughed as Dimitri headed back out and continued down the street, passing by the coffee shop that was the central meeting place for the neighborhood's senior citizens.

*   *   *

Unlike the swanky and hip coffee shops of uptown Hamra Street, Abo Fareed's place was a traditional small neighborhood shop, more of a social club where pensioners gathered around tables playing *tawli* (backgammon) or cards while drinking coffee, smoking, joking and ranting. Periodically, a heated debate would break out, only to be followed by raucous laughter after Abo Karam, the resident philosopher, would highlight the valid points and simultaneously the absurdities of both sides of the argument. He would always end by saying: "*Yalla! Yalla!* We don't have many seasons left in us to spend arguing. *Yalla! Yalla! ta' nilaab.*" (Come on! Come on! Let's play). And the roll of the dice would keep the old men's spirits moving along with a rejuvenated sense of purpose that comes from daily social exchanges between old friends. The old men's wives were happy to have their husbands out of the house as well, so they could enjoy their own social rituals of inviting each other for tea, sweets and conversation.

The first item on Teta's list was bread. Dimitri crossed the street and went into the baker's alley, full of the aroma of fresh baked goods. Midway through the alley, he turned right and entered a nondescript door that led down a flight of steps into a cavernous space housing a commercial masonry oven, radiating heat and putting out a deep orange glow into the room.

The bakery was owned and run by Abo Toni and his son Toni, who presided over the oven with a two-meter spatula designed to deliver six round pita bread loaves into the oven at a time, then swiftly scoop up and remove half a dozen loaves that were already baked to golden perfection. With the tilt of the spatula, he placed the loaves on a cooling table to be packaged by the dozen. Without missing a beat, Toni would swiftly move on to deliver another six loaves into the fiery pit with all the finesse of a bakery maestro.

Dimitri picked up a dozen loaves of pita and, with a "*Shukran!*" thanked Abo Toni, who responded with "*Sahtein!*" Literally translated, this means *two healths:* one is added for good measure, to express generous wishes for good health to the recipient.

Teta always said, "The baker does God's work. "Dimitri also heard her say on occasion, "In times of abundance, bread is the foundation, and in times of famine, bread is the savior." Teta had sayings that Dimitri didn't fully understand. But he understood the part about doing God's work by providing the people with their daily bread.

Bread has a special cultural importance for the Lebanese, especially those who experienced the famine of the First World War. Teta was a child at the time. Thanks to her parents' resilience and luck, they were spared the terrible fate of the more than 200,000 people who starved to death in Mount Lebanon. The Mount Lebanon famine produced one of the highest fatality rates per capita during the First World War, alongside the Armenian genocide, Assyrian genocide and Greek genocide.

As the Ottoman Empire began to fall, the Ottomans adopted a severe policy of acquisition, by which all food supplies were prioritized for their army. Jamal Pasha barred crops from entering Mount Lebanon. One-third of the population perished, while another third migrated. Only a third survived and remained in the villages of Mount Lebanon. It was a catastrophic chapter in the history of the country, as well as the region. Half a century later, food insecurity remained a concern in the back of Lebanese minds. During the economic boom of the golden age, a kind of monument to food security was built at the port of Beirut: a giant state-of-the-art cluster of 42 wheat silos holding 120,000 metric tons of wheat, standing as a functional symbol of food security.

Dimitri walked out of the baker's alley onto the next city block, heading down towards the butcher shop. Midway, he passed by Antwan, who was polishing his car outside the neighborhood taxi station. Antwan's son Fadi was one of Dimitri's friends and a fellow neighborhood footballer.

"*Marhaba Maalem* Antwan," Dimitri called out. Antwan, who was obsessively polishing his car, looked up.

"*Ahleeein ya* Dimitri! Welcome back. Fadi is at the football field with his friends. He will be happy to see you." With his momentum flowing, Antwan didn't skip a beat as he continued methodically polishing the Mercedes 180 Ponton that provided the livelihood for his family.

The neighborhood's taxi station consisted of an office with a garage and workshop. It was the nerve center and intelligence-gathering hub of the area, keeping tabs on the who, what, where, comings and goings of the city, all in real time. It was said that if you really want to know the latest news on the street, ask a taxi driver; they always had their finger on the pulse of the city.

The proprietor, Elie, ran his station from his desk, with two telephones flanking him. The center of the desk remained clear and open, to accommodate a backgammon *tawli* set and coffee for his friends. Elie ran his fleet like a commander moving supplies and personnel through the maze of streets and alleys of Beirut. He had two old friends from his army days who worked with him as part-time drivers for the VIPs, which meant the neighborhood's elderly who needed a ride to the doctor or to pick up a special guest from the airport. They were semi-retired army pensioners who spent most of their time with Elie playing *tawli*, drinking coffee, smoking and talking politics.

Four other cars were driven by reliable middle-aged family men providing for their families. Among them was Fadi's father, Antwan. They had been with Elie for years. They could be chatty or silent depending on the social cues of their passengers. They were professionals hired and trained by Elie.

Two other vans were driven by single young men he had recruited. They were given assignments that involved transporting goods in vans, mostly crates from the Beirut port. They were chosen for being strong, fit, disciplined, reliable and loyal. They were also street smart and in tune with the pulse and rhythms of the city and its underworld. They were armed and thus held a constant fascination for the kids of the neighborhood, who would often describe tales of adventure, danger and heroics attributed to them, some of them even true.

In the past, during the 19th century, Beirut had enjoyed a very effective public transportation system, with an electric street rail program like those of San Francisco and Paris. With the advent of the 20th century, taxis became a big part of the city's culture, as in London and New York.

The Mercedes 180 Ponton was the quintessential reliable Beirut taxicab, with an engine that went on forever.

Each driver adorned his vehicle with custom decorations embellished with thistles and medallions. A variety of postcard images of Lebanon were displayed in a collage on the dashboard. An evil-eye medallion to ward off the spirits of those with ill intentions hung from the rearview mirror, along with a medallion of Saint Michael, the patron saint of safe travel. The car radio played on, while the car horn doubled as a punctuating musical instrument.

Car horns also served as a means of communication between the driver and pedestrians and other vehicles.

The horn had a range in the way it was used depending on the circumstance. A brief, gentle touch honk to say thank you, or the more forceful but still brief question-mark horn, accompanied with a turning of the wrist and fingers. Two crisp bursts requested an opportunity to pass. Persistent short bursts called for attention. Then, finally, there was the big blast, accompanied by profanities, to keep the traffic moving. All were part of the mix of the noisy, busy streets of Beirut.

Crossing the street onto the next city block, Dimitri passed by the neighborhood bookstore, a place entered quietly with a sense of respect and consideration for its proprietor and thoughtful customers. On entering the store, the smell of fresh ink on paper from the dailies and periodicals was a welcoming smell, signaling that one might learn something new today. The bookstore was an oasis of calmness, discovery and reflection amid the noisy city.

The owner, Maalem Emile, was the son of a history professor, who grew up with books. Emile was now in his fifties and had quite a collection of books in a variety of genres. He had a special locked bookcase that housed an extensive collection of first editions. On top of the bookcase behind his desk sat the mascot of the bookstore, a cat named Socrates, who seemed to live in a world of his own. Through his peripheral vision, he kept a watchful eye on the street outside with its comings and goings and the customers entering the store, whom he appeared to totally ignore while remaining aware of their every move.

Socrates would come down from his perch when Dimitri visited the store. The two were old friends. After being petted on the head and cheeks, the nimble feline would leap up to the top of the bookcase again, curling up and gazing into another world. Maalem Emile called this "contemplation."

In a quiet, peaceful area of the bookstore was a special section that supported local writers and poets. Dimitri's older cousin Anthony's book of poetry stood there, along with other locally written books on history, politics, novels and short stories.

At the far corner of the shop were two large, flat files housing limited-edition prints, lithographs and antique maps. Some of the maps were centuries old, dating from the early days of the printing press. Some even older ones were rendered with ink on paper.

Dimitri had been coming into the bookstore with Teta since he was a little child, when he would head straight to the comic book section while Teta bought her daily *Al Nahar* newspaper. Dimitri later developed other interests, among them history and maps.

Maalem Emile would bring out some of the oldest maps in his collection, which were protected in acid-free archival sleeves. He would point out details on the maps to Dimitri and Teta, saying, "See, Lebanon! It always was and always will be." Dimitri would respond with "*Yaeesh Lubnan!*" (Long live Lebanon!) Teta and Maalem Emile, nodding their heads and smiling in approval, would both call out a "*Yaeesh Lubnan!*" of their own.

Tourists would often walk into the bookstore and be greeted graciously by Maalem Emile, who would direct them to his extensive collection of books on Lebanese history and antiquities. "Please enjoy and let me know if I can help you," he would say as he gently bowed away, leaving the tourists to look over the books and the tour brochures strategically placed next to them. The brochures were from the travel agency on the floor above the bookstore, run by his sister Jackline, who arranged tours of historical sites with Elie's VIP neighborhood taxi service.

Even in the thoughtful intellectual world, making connections and engaging in commerce is a deeply ingrained trait of Lebanese culture. This is often attributed to their ancient Phoenician ancestors, known as the great traders of the Mediterranean. Trading and commerce remain a deep part of the culture in large part due to the geographical location of Lebanon between East and West, which made it a natural business hub throughout history.

*　　*　　*

Next to the bookstore was one of Dimitri's favorite shops. He called it the "shop of memories." The photography studio was owned and run by Hovik, who as a child had fled with his father, mother and two siblings from Armenia during the Ottoman genocide of the Armenian people. In Beirut, the family found refuge, safety and acceptance by the Lebanese.

Hovik's business was a small portrait studio with a darkroom for developing film and printing photographs. He also sold cameras and Kodak film to photography enthusiasts, tourists and foreign photojournalists. On his lunch break, Hovik walked the streets of the busy city, photographing daily life. Like many who have experienced loss, Hovik was fascinated by photography at an early age, when he realized the amazing power of this magic box called a camera: a box that could capture a place and a time and preserve it forever in a photograph.

Long after Hovik, future generations would see his photographic work as a window in time, reflecting a bygone era that could still be visited in one of his prints. His photographs were not simply static studies with a camera; they evoked the atmosphere and spirit of the places and people he had photographed, giving the viewer a sense of being there in that long-ago time and space.

Dimitri had a similar fascination with photography. When he was four years old, he took his first photograph with a Kodak Brownie camera. It was a picture of his father smiling at him. The photograph was taken three months before his father unexpectedly died. Now, his father continued to smile at him from the frame on the wall, a man in his thirties at what should have been the peak of his life. He was happily smiling while looking affectionately and optimistically toward the future, in the form of his four-year-old son taking a picture of him.

Dimitri would often look at that picture and find a tear running down his cheek over a smile. As the years passed, the photograph of his father shared space with posters of race cars, sports heroes, action movie stars and an assortment of other teenage interests and fascinations. Life had moved on, and while the absence of his father during those formative early years left an emotional scar, his mother, uncles, aunts, and above all Teta and her brother, the old stonemason Saleem, had a profound influence on his growth and his outlook on life.

*   *   *

As Dimitri continued his walk through the neighborhood, he passed by Abo Khalil's movie theater. An uncontrollable giggle overcame him as he recalled some of the highlights at the movies with his neighborhood friends. Movie theaters were a big part of Beirut's culture. For centuries, the port of Beirut had been a window and a portal to the rest of the world.

Now, with the advent of film in the late 19th century, the movies were yet another way to connect with the broader world. Many Beirut businessmen with a worldly view and a knack for making money opened movie theaters across the city. The Roxy, Empire, Rivoli, Piccadilly, Commodore, Odeon, Strand, Citi Palace, Hamra, Concorde and Starco, to name a few, were grand and opulent, some with crystal chandeliers and plush velvet seats.

The weekends saw premieres with night skylights beaming into the heavens announcing the first release of a new French, American or Egyptian movie. Families and moviegoers wore their best clothes for the occasion. The grand theaters were places to see and be seen. When the ruffled burgundy red curtain trimmed in gold, opened and the lights of the chandelier went dark, the audience would be transported on a two-hour journey to another world through the magic of the silver screen.

The smaller neighborhood movie theaters had their own magic for a lower ticket price and a more casual atmosphere. Abo Khalil's theater was sparse, with folding chairs and a concrete floor. It was not uncommon to hear Abo Khalil call out to the audience during an afternoon screening, "Lift your feet up; a bucket of water is coming your way." Abo Khalil often cleaned his theater at the end of the Friday afternoon show in preparation for the weekend main events.

Abo Khalil had been a merchant marine in his younger years, working on commercial ships that took him around the world. He had visited all the major ports and cities before he turned 45 and decided to return home to settle down and open a neighborhood movie theater in the building below his apartment. On Friday afternoons, Abo Khalil would run a spaghetti-western double feature from his extensive collection of B-movie reels. The neighborhood kids would all head to the theater and for fifty piasters were treated to B-movie westerns where mayhem would play out on the screen with the kids turning the theater into an interactive, joyful place filled with commentary, raucous laughter, curses, boos, clapping and cheering at the screen.

*   *   *

Dimitri had a couple of more stops to make before arriving at the neighborhood football field. The butcher shop was next to his uncle's store, two blocks from the theater. The neighborhood butcher, Shirbil, was a serious, quiet and stoic sort of fellow. Every morning, as Dimitri walked to school with his friends, they would pass by the sheep tied by the shop's side door in the alley. The sheep must have felt they had hit the jackpot as they feasted on a pile of fresh green remnants that the next-door greengrocer placed for them in two piles after arranging his shop's display for the day. On Dimitri's way back home from school, he would see the severed heads of the butchered sheep in the chilled display case facing the shop window, staring out at the pedestrians passing by. Next to the heads would be a piece of cardboard with the price of sheep brains marked on it. Other parts of the sheep carcasses hung from hooks. the choicest cuts having been carved out and bought up early by the neighborhood families for their dinner stews.

Shirbil stood over a meat grinder, churning out the remnants of the carcasses, which would be mixed with his special blend of fresh spices and pine nuts. He would funnel the mixture into the casings: intestines that had been cleaned and flushed with salt water. Every ten centimeters, he would give the casing a twist, thus tying both ends of each sausage, before repeating the process to create a large necklace of the best sausages in town.

Dimitri stopped by Shirbil's shop and picked up a kilo of sausages before heading to his uncle George's store next door for eggs and cheese.

George was happy to see Dimitri back. After catching him up on the neighborhood stories of the past two months, George asked, "Now that you're back, are you ready to make some money and start helping Sammy deliver propane tanks?"

"Yes, of course. I can start on Monday."

Dimitri headed up the street towards the neighborhood football field and turned the corner, where he saw Fadi, Elie, Andre, Toni, Gerious, Gibran, Hasan, Waleed, Rasheed, Ali, Saleh, Ishak and Rafi, who let out a collective joyful cheer of a welcome that he reciprocated affectionately, with hugs and the traditional three kisses on alternating cheeks.

"*Yala*, come on, let's play," said Andre. "Toni, Riad, Paul, Mohamad, Yohanna, Nader, Rasheed and the others will be here soon."

"I can't today. We just got back, and I must help Teta," said Dimitri, "but I'll be out here early tomorrow."

"*Azeem!*" Fadi yelled out to the departing Dimitri "We will tell everyone to meet on the field tomorrow morning."

The football field was the most integrated piece of land in the neighborhood. It was one of the few remaining open large spaces in the city, situated at the meeting point of three different, rapidly growing neighborhoods of different ethnicities. Christian, Muslim, Jewish Lebanese kids as well as Armenian, Kurd and Palestinians all congregated on the field, interacting and playing memorable games that unbeknown to them at the time created joyful memories of childhood and youth that would stay with them for a lifetime.

The football field was also a gathering place. The little kids played with marbles, while the youth played *Shaki,* a knife throwing game. Others gathered and shared the latest stories, hatched plans and played some of the best football in town, thanks to Ali, the football child phenom.

During summer, Ali spent all day on the football field. He took a break only for lunch and would seldom join his friends on bike tours or fishing and diving trips to the sea. Ali was the brother of six siblings, with many family obligations that always kept him close to home. Luckily, the football field was within earshot of his mother, who often summoned him from the balcony overlooking the field.

Ali was passionate, focused, and obsessed with football. To him, football was life. His sister Fatemeh had a condition that kept her in a wheelchair. Ali was her caretaker and driver, pushing her wheelchair to and from school. Fatemeh loved her older brother and was his biggest fan. She was often at the football field in her chair, cheering her brother during the games and even while he practiced by himself against an imaginary team. Fatemeh would often tell her brother how much joy it gave her to watch him play. "It's as if I am out of this chair and playing myself."

Ali was a wizard with the ball, making it seem to momentarily disappear and reappear. He was light on his feet and could shift directions at surprising speed and at seemingly impossible angles. One moment he was here, the next he was there. And while his opponents were still trying to react, he was already a move or two ahead of them. Ali was brilliant. He was able to read the fluid play on the field with what seemed like an extra sense of awareness. He knew where his opponents and his teammates were at all times, and was anywhere from a fraction of a second to a few seconds ahead of everyone, seeing windows of opportunity before they even opened. He seemed to be playing under the physics of a different time dilation, allowing him to anticipate and make moves that the opposing team had to catch up with. It was as if he was a clairvoyant seer on the field. His fast-twitch muscles and his brain were wired for the sport. And his heart was fully in love with and dedicated to the beautiful game. He was a joy to watch and was known in the neighborhood as "little Rivellino" after the legendary Brazilian footballer who was a master magician and an amazing athlete of his time.

*   *   *

The neighborhood football field once had an old house on it, with a large garden and a water fountain visited by birds that would refresh themselves while whistling and singing their songs of gratitude. The garden's seating area had four old grapevines that rose and twisted together forming a leafy canopy that gave shade to its residents during summer. The old house was inherited by an expatriate living in Argentina who sold it and the surrounding property to a developer who tore the old house down for a future project of a cluster of steel and concrete buildings, like the many emerging all over the city.

The neighborhood's old residents lamented the destruction of the beautiful old home that had been so much a part of the history and character of the neighborhood. The passage of time leaves behind people who still remember a bygone era with nostalgia, while the new generation goes on with ambitious quests and busy lives, oblivious to the rich history beneath their feet. In time, the same piece of land would be transformed yet again, with new lives and memories attached to it.

Someday Dimitri and his friends would feel the same nostalgia in remembering the joyful times spent on that once open field, destined to become a cluster of buildings and alleys filled with new generations making memories of their own. For better or worse, life only moves forward.

*   *   *

Dimitri walked up the hill, heading home with his bag of groceries. On the way, he came across Abo Ghazi, pushing his cart with a large mound of okra on display while calling out the virtues of his fresh product available at a special price. Unlike some pushcart vendors, often considered a nuisance, Abo Ghazi had an operatic voice that made his call entertaining to all who heard it.

Pushcart vendors are an enterprising group. When a fruit or vegetable is in season, Abo Ghazi would buy in bulk from the wholesale market downtown and sell his goods for retail along the streets and alleys of the city.

As the pushcart vendor passed by in the street below, the customer would call out to him from a balcony. After a deal was agreed upon, the customer would lower a rope with a bamboo basket containing the payment, which the vendor exchanged for whatever the cook wanted: fresh produce, vegetables, nuts, legumes, etc. The basket of fresh food was then pulled up to the balcony, only a few steps away from the kitchen.

While Dimitri was out running his errands, Teta had pulled up a basket of okra from Abo Ghazi's pushcart. Uncle Victor had set up an electric pulley system for Teta when she moved from the traditional three-story masonry building of her young adult life to a modern seven-story apartment building with an elevator to live with Samira and Dimitri. For the longest time, Teta insisted on pulling up the basket with her own two hands. She still did occasionally, if it wasn't a heavy load. But she had found the electric pulley to be a practical and necessary convenience in her senior years.

After dinner and unpacking from the stay in the mountains, Dimitri turned the lights off in his room and lay down on his bed listening to the city sounds: car horns, sirens, someone stumbling in the alley, a neighbor yelling at a drunk, alley cats mating, and an assortment of other city sounds that composed the familiar background soundtrack, one he hadn't heard in a while.

City sounds were quite different from the peace and quiet of Dimitri's beloved mountains. Even so, he had missed them, and missed his neighborhood. Staring up at the dark ceiling and lost in thought, he saw the light from the Beirut lighthouse panning across the wall. It would repeat its illuminating visit across the dark walls every two minutes. Most residents would draw their blinds at what they considered a nuisance, but Dimitri welcomed it. He drifted to sleep with a smile on his face, thinking happily of playing football and seeing all his neighborhood friends on the field the next day.

*   *   *

At dusk, the distant sound of the *Athan* from the mosque on the other side of downtown traveled through the still sleeping and silent city. The muezzin's voice was beautiful, earthy and heavenly at the same time, ascending and descending while calling the faithful to prayer and giving tribute, praise and thanks for a new God-given day. The masterful recital by a beautiful voice was peaceful and hopeful, and everyone in the surrounding area welcomed this beautiful and gentle beginning of their day, regardless of their religion.

After a while, other calls to prayer chimed in, some through bullhorns. They were different. They were aggressive, harsh, loud, jarring and urgent. Then the mechanized sounds of engines, mixed in with the constant and persistent horns of the taxis, started to make their rounds. The city was up, and the hustle and bustle had begun.

*   *   *

After breakfast, Dimitri was fueled for the start of the day and excitedly headed to the football field. There was Ali, putting on a skill show for his friends with his spectacular moves and dribbles. Warm greetings were exchanged by all before the game. After the requisite bantering between friends, the whistle blew a piercing sound, and the game was on. It started conservatively, with well-measured passes, until Ali got the ball and started his magic. Every time he passed by an opponent, players on both teams would shake their heads in disbelief and admiration at his skills. Dimitri played half back and was known for his rocket-launcher foot, scoring from a distance into the upper corner of the goal. Nader, the goalkeeper, came up with many formidable and inspiring saves, many of them while diving and flying into the air with acrobatic flair to nudge the ball out of its scoring trajectory.

There is no reunion more joyful and exhilarating than that of a football game among old friends. And so, it was on this beautiful blue-sky summer day in Beirut.

Tour de Beirut

After lunch, the neighborhood friends gathered at the field. When everyone was accounted for, they got on their bikes and began pumping the pedals through two alleys and on to the main road of Corniche Pierre Gemayel, which led to the Beirut-Damascus highway. The pack remained in single file while a caravan of large freight trucks loaded with goods from the Beirut port flew by them towards their destination over two mountain passes before reaching Damascus, and from there further east into Iraq and the desert states. Plumes of dust mixed with the thick diesel exhaust filled the air.

The pack of friends remained disciplined and in single file for the long stretch of the Beirut-Damascus highway until they arrived at a turning point where the route veered off to the right and into the Beirut pine forest. Then they cruised along, occasionally passing each other while exchanging observations, tips and plans for navigating the streets and neighborhoods ahead.

The focus of the day was the fishing trap they were going to pick up from Abo Rasheed's workshop at the downtown fish market. The friends had been saving up and pooled their money for this partnership.

After cruising a while under the shade of the pines, that gave a welcome respite from the sun, sweat and grit of the Beirut-Damascus highway stage. They arrived at Abo Abed's juice bar and refueled their bodies with carrot, mango, apple, orange, watermelon and fresh sugarcane water, derived from sugarcane shoots fed into a peeling, grinding and pulverizing contraption that produced pure, sweet sugarcane juice.

Feeling energized and refreshed, the friends hopped on their bikes and pedaled on into an open space, with white sand as far as the eye could see. The area was called *Ramlet el bayda*, and its vast open space of white sands extended all the way south towards the airport and west to the Mediterranean Sea. Already there were plans to develop this pristine expanse of open space. The main roads had been built and plots of land demarcated. Peddling towards the sea, they came to a newly built, double-level, four-lane paved road along the coast. It was a perfectly flat and straight stretch that looked more like an airport runway. The upper level was packed with spectators for the weekend drag races, some sitting off the edge of the second level while dangling their legs from the front row above the race strip below. Beirut's top mechanic shops brought their prized, big-block, American muscle cars out to the strip: the Chevy Chevelle SS, GTO, Oldsmobile 442, Dodge Charger, Pontiac Trans Am, Chevrolet Camaro, Ford Mustang, and some unassuming sleepers. One sleeper in particular, a favorite of Dimitri, was the unassuming Duster that Abo Raymon, the neighborhood ace mechanic at Elie's taxi service, brought out every weekend to the race strip. The cars were all enhanced with the latest technology, from nitro boosters to Holley double pumper carburetors and Hurst shifters.

The boys got off their bikes and watched a few races, charging them with adrenaline. Continuing their bike tour, they pedaled hard with a great deal of torque, climbing up a curving hill that led to a long stretch of Beirut's Raouche, overlooking the Pigeon Rocks, where they settled into a leisurely cruise, enjoying the view and taking in the fresh sea breeze while giving their pumping hearts time to settle down before the next stage of the tour.

Cruising past the Pigeon Rocks lagoon, they arrived at a string of seaside cafes where the aroma of freshly brewed coffee, cardamom and tobacco filled the air. The raspy voices of old men engaged in a passionate game of *tawli* mixed with the sound of rapidly thrown dice and backgammon pieces being slammed on the table with gusto in a dramatic assertion of success, followed by bantering, laughter and more trickling of the dice.

Coasting down the winding road to the beginning of the Corniche, with the wind flowing through their hair and the sea breeze filling their lungs, they passed the Beirut lighthouse, perched atop a hill, with Beirut's iconic Rose House at its base. The Rose House mansion once housed foreigners who loved Beirut and made it their home. Among them was abstract painter John Ferren, one of Picasso's close friends and his canvas preparer. There were also several American professors who taught at the American University of Beirut and historical dignitaries such as France's General Charles De Gaulle. The mansion overlooked clay tennis courts and from its balconies offered a spectacular view of the dramatic Mediterranean sunsets.

The old lighthouse had guided countless ships to safe harbor at the Beirut port and had been part of the nightly ritual of many Beirut residents falling asleep on summer nights with the windows open. As the light from the lighthouse made its complete rotation around the ancient city every two minutes, illuminating the buildings and apartments in its path.

The lighthouse marked the starting point of a sprint among the friends and cyclists, who pumped the pedals and flew by the many sea-gazers who were gathered along the railing of the Corniche overlooking the sea, sipping beverages and eating *bascoti* or *kake* from one of the many vendors posted along the Corniche.

Two men, friends since childhood, stood savoring their coffee next to Abo Naeem, the coffee vendor. "Look, look," said one to the other, observing the youths on their bikes. "That was us, decades ago."

"*Eih walla,*" that is true, answered his friend wistfully. "*Rizk alla ala hal ayam.* Memorable days, my friend; those were days of innocence and joy."

"They certainly were. Time slips through our hands like sand. Yesterday we were 16; today we are 66. Just like that, half a century has passed. We have been so busy with work, our families and life, while the years pass by like clouds in the sky." The two old friends lifted their coffee cups, savoring another sip as they looked out to the horizon.

The young cyclists all made it to the finish line, which was Abo Ali's *jallab* stand, across the street from the American University of Beirut's greenfield sea gate. Students on break from their studies and families taking a walk on the Corniche stopped by Abo Ali's *jallab* stand and enjoyed his special refreshment while watching the fishermen cast their lines into the sea.

Here, the friends dismounted and refueled with the traditional Lebanese drink made of grape molasses, dates and rose water, garnished with pine nuts and raisins, then served over shaved ice in a large, frosty glass mug.

Abo Ali had established himself with the finest ingredients and a recipe made fresh daily at dawn. The *jallab* was stored in insulated, ornate silver-plated vats, hand-hammered works of art finely crafted by the multigenerational silver, copper and brass artisans of Tripoli, on the northern coast of Lebanon.

Abo Ali wore a spotless white apron, with a few folded spares kept in a bin underneath his pushcart stand. He prepared his beverages with efficiency, precision and a flair that was entertaining to watch. He began by shaving the ice with the speed and precision of a prize fighter working a speed bag. Then he poured the *jallab*, garnished it with raisins and pine nuts, and delivered it to his customers with a blessing of *"Sahtein!"* (Two healths!), topped off with a warm smile. Abo Ali was a proud man with a bright spirit who never missed a chance to tell customers that his son is at the top of his class and, God willing, would be a student at the university in the future.

The friends savored their *jallab* as they marveled at the campus, perched atop a hill overlooking the sea. While respecting and preserving the past, the university continued to graduate the top doctors, engineers, architects, writers, philosophers, historians and businesswomen and men in the Middle East, many of whom have risen to international acclaim in their field. The campus was founded by American Protestant missionaries in the mid 1800s and opened its main gate to higher learning in 1866, with Daniel Bliss as one of its main founders and its first president. His vision was for a premier learning institution that accepted students from all backgrounds and religions. The university's alumni have had a significant impact on the region and the world.

Master stonemasons were purposely hired by the missionaries to include masons of all religions, among them Dimitri's ancestors. The stone chapel, watchtower and classroom buildings were topped with red ceramic tile roofs and surrounded by trees and gardens. A.U.B. remained a beautifully preserved part of Beirut's past, standing in contrast to the concrete, steel and glass structures that have taken over the cityscape.

From the Corniche gate of the university, the friends slowly cruised past the American Embassy and into the hotel district, where they dismounted for a while to watch the water-ski show from the free public promenade overlooking the Hotel Saint George, a swanky hotel filled with international jetsetters sipping cocktails in fancy sun hats and bikinis. Cigar smoke mixed with the salty sea breeze as fat cats of business and spies working for the intelligence agencies of the West and East intermingled in this exclusive setting while making connections, hatching profitable deals and making sinister plans.

A spectacular water-ski show was on display, with the finest handcrafted wooden powerboats cutting through the blue sea while towing professional water-skiers at high speed, slinging them airborne over floating launching ramps. One of the skiers that caught Dimitri's eye was a beautiful, naturally athletic woman with a sweet yet confident look. Seeing her gliding expertly on the surface of the deep blue water mesmerized Dimitri into a 16-year-old's hypnotized state of infatuation. Every time she passed by his heart was filled with deep admiration.

The powerful 255 horsepower inboard marine Waukesha engine inside the all-wood pleasure craft rumbled as it towed her out to sea and boomeranged her in a slow, wide arc across the horizon before heading back at high speed towards him. The distant rumble grew louder as she approached, and with-it Dimitri's heart sped up and roared in unison. The powerful craft glided across the blue sea and slung the skier up and off the ramp, where she became momentarily airborne and soaring. At that moment, Dimitri saw everything in slow motion; he imagined himself in a glorious embrace with the enchanting skier, flying together into the sun of a true-blue sky.

As she landed her jump, the crowd's roar of applause brought him back to reality, feeling a bit dazed and confused. When the boat returned to the marina, the water-skier ran into the waiting embrace of her lover.

Dimitri let out a deep, disappointed sigh. "*Yala*, let's go," he said, and with that the boys hopped on their bikes and pumped the pedals up Fakhreddine Street, past the Phoenicia and Holiday Inn hotels, before turning left into the Jewish neighborhood of Wadi Abou Jamil (Valley of the Father of Beauty). There they passed the Maghen Abraham Synagogue and proceeded through a maze of streets and alleys heading towards downtown Beirut. Along the way, they passed by the Prince Monzer Mosque before turning onto Emir Bechir Street and arriving at Saint George's Cathedral, at the entrance to Martyrs' Square. The celebrated religious diversity of Beirut was evident throughout their journey, as they passed by synagogues, churches and mosques while weaving through the neighborhood streets and alleys leading into the heart of the city.

Downtown Beirut

The streets of downtown Beirut were densely packed with cars, buses, motorcycles, bicycles, pedestrians and a wide array of mobile vendors selling *Kaek*, refreshments, snacks and coffee to keep the frantic pace going. Standing in the middle of it all was a traffic policeman presiding over interweaving waves of traffic and pedestrians, directing them all with dramatic hand gestures punctuated with piercing blasts from a whistle that had a wide range of melodic effects, all intended to keep the flow going. The traffic policeman's constant gestures and whistles were taken as no more than suggestions by the motorists and pedestrians weaving through traffic.

It has been said that traffic in Berlin, Germany, is as orderly as a symphony orchestra; Beirut's traffic, in contrast, was a spontaneous jazz jam session filled with complex harmonies, syncopated rhythms, and a heavy emphasis on improvisation.

Entering the city center at Martyrs' Square, the friends merged into traffic filled with taxis and buses. Navigating through it all, they arrived at the marble steps that led up to the iconic statue at the center of the square, where they rested and regrouped while taking in the theater of life unfolding around them. Martyrs' Square was two blocks from the Beirut port and the commercial center and transportation hub of the country, with streets emanating from it in several directions. From here, buses, trucks and taxis took passengers and goods to all parts of the country and neighboring Syria and on from Damascus into the Iraqi desert towards Asia.

The square was surrounded by commercial buildings, offices, theaters, restaurants, souks and bazaars. In the center stood a bronze statue of a strong, determined woman, holding a torch with her right arm in front of her, while embracing a Lebanese youth with her other arm and leading him with the light of the torch forward to a brighter future. At their feet were statues of fallen Lebanese Nationalists of different religions who together resisted and revolted against the oppressive Ottoman Empire.

After 300 years of occupation and oppression, the Ottoman Empire had fallen, and the statue was erected after independence as a tribute to the Nationalists who had been executed on the very same spot. Dimitri, Fadi, Elie, Marwan, Ramzi, Baha, Ishak, Ghaleb and Antwan gathered at the base of the statue, where they counted out their money and gave it to Dimitri in preparation for entering Abo Rasheed's workshop deep in the fish market to buy a professional hand-crafted fish trap.

The friends made their way into the fish market, walking their bikes in single file with Dimitri in the lead, using his bicycle bell along with a polite *"min fadlak"* (if you please) asking people obstructing the pathway of human traffic to clear the way. The degree of force applied to the ring of the bell and the tone of the *"min fadlak"* spanned from a gentle and polite request to a more aggressive and urgent command, depending on the circumstances. It was not unlike the vehicular traffic, where taxi drivers used their horns as an instrument of communication, along with verbal exchanges ranging in tone from poetic sweetness to curses of unimaginable profanity, depending on the circumstances.

The friends strolled along, marveling at the wide array of fish and sea creatures on display, making their way to Abo Rasheed's workshop. They leaned their bikes against the wall of the shop, next to the old, weathered wooden doors, with a rusty cast-iron door knocker molded in the shape of a human hand holding a solid iron sphere.

Dimitri lifted the heavy knocker and let it tap twice before the friends entered. A deep, warm but scratchy voice greeted them: *"Ahlan bil sayadeen*" (welcome, fishermen). Abo Rasheed was in the middle of masterfully weaving one of the fine fishing nets he was acclaimed for. He asked his apprentice to help the young fishermen with what they needed and returned to his focused, meditative work.

Dimitri explained to the apprentice that they were interested in buying a professional, handmade wire fish trap. The apprentice pointed to a section of the wall with rusty traps on display and said, "These here are very good and sell for 15 Lebanese pounds."

"What about these shiny new ones over there?" asked Fadi.

"They are new and are only 10 Lebanese pounds."

The friends huddled together to discuss the alternatives and concluded that the apprentice was confused and didn't know what he was talking about. How could a brand new, shiny trap be less expensive than an old, rusty one? Without asking further questions, the shrewd young business partners struck while the iron was hot.

"Ten Lebanese pounds; we will take that new one there."

The new trap was fastened with wire to Dimitri's handlebars, and the group of friends headed out of the fish market, ecstatic at the great deal they had scored. Heading back to their neighborhood, they were giddy with optimism for tomorrow's fishing trip, each of them calling out what kind of fish they hoped to catch for tomorrow's dinner.

"Marmoora," yelled Dimitri.

"Sargoos," replied Marwan.

"Boori," said Antwan.

"Sultan Abrahim," answered Baha.

"Lahaj … haddad …barak …rayes," the list went on, with the friends all calling out names of the abundant array of fish off the coast of Beirut. The cyclists continued to weave through traffic until they began peeling off from the pack as they approached home, calling out to the remaining friends, "*Tusbahoo ala kheir*" (awake to goodness), and the rest of the pack responding in kind.

The young fishermen

A new day dawned with the sounds of the city coming back to life: taxi horns seeking customers' attention; pushcart vendors calling out their fresh produce to the early balcony shoppers, *"Yalla al Banadoora!!!"* Up the street, a compressor fired up its diesel engine for the jackhammers working on repaving a street. Smells of diesel and melting asphalt started to fill the air.

The friends began gathering at the football field with their fishing poles strapped to their bikes. The poles were handmade the traditional way, with three carefully chosen shoots of bamboo cut to two meters each, then customized to fit with each other by working the ends with a pocketknife, shaving them for a precision snug fit to produce a sturdy, light and flexible 6-meter fishing pole. The tip was given a crosscut and the line crisscrossed through and tied into a knot. A cork floater, lead sinker and hook completed the simple, handmade tool that had fed and sustained human life from the sea's abundance along the coasts of the world for thousands of years.

Fueled with a *manouche* each from Abo Toni's neighborhood bakery, the friends began to cruise on their bikes towards the sea. As they approached the rocky shore, they dismounted and walked down the hill on a path towards the water's edge, brushing up against wild thyme bushes along the way. Each picked a spot on the shore to post and assemble their poles and placed their baskets in one of the many shallow pools that dotted the rocky shoreline. The half-submerged baskets were meant to keep their catch alive and fresh until the end of the day, when they would pick them up and head home.

The sound of gentle waves washing over the shore was soothing, their ebb and flow regulating an inner rhythm that cleared the mind and calmed the soul.

With everything in place on shore, the friends gathered to sing a fishermen's song in praise of fishing and friendship before taking the inaugural plunge with the shiny new fish trap. Expectations were high for Abo Rasheed's finely crafted trap, which reflected the sun's rays like a silver metal sculpture of a shimmering star. The friends were all familiar with the depths and terrain of the wonderland beneath the surface. There was a particular spot that formed a kind of underwater lagoon frequented by whole schools of fish. Its walls were gnarly rock formations dotted with sea urchins and cavernous homes for octopuses and eels. The bottom floor, eight meters down, was sandy and clear.

The friends dived in and swam out, with Dimitri and Fadi, the two strongest swimmers, holding the baited trap. When they reached their destination, Dimitri dived down and placed it on the sandy floor before slowly floating back up to the surface and giving the thumbs-up sign to the rest of the crew. With the trap baited and in place, they all swam back together to start their day of fishing, diving and swimming off Beirut's rocky coast.

The day was going well for the young fishermen, who were all pulling in their share of fish with their handmade bamboo poles. Every hour or so, one of them would swim out to check on the trap, only to return and share the disappointing news of it being empty. At the end of the day, as the sun began its descent, Dimitri and Fadi swam out to retrieve the trap. The friends were all happy after a summer day of swimming, diving and fishing. But they were also puzzled and disappointed that their prized new trap hadn't captured a single fish.

*   *   *

When they got to shore, they saw an old man setting up his fishing post with a lantern in preparation for night fishing. *"Shoo ya shabab?* Hey young men, how is the fishing today?" he yelled out.

"We all caught some good ones offshore, but the trap caught nothing," said Dimitri.

"I see your problem," said the old fisherman. "Your trap is new and shiny, and the fish will avoid it. It is, however, a fine trap, expertly made. Who made it?"

"It's from Abo Rasheed, downtown," Dimitri responded.

"I thought so. Abo Rasheed is an old friend and a good man. I'm sure you could turn in your new shiny trap for a well-seasoned one. It will cost you a little more."

The friends all thanked the old man. *"Shukran ya maalem,"* and wished him good luck on his night fishing.

Now they recalled the old rusty traps with a higher price and understood why they had cost more than the new shiny ones. It was a lesson that not everything new and shiny is desirable or useful. Some things get better with age, after they have seen many seasons pass.

Another trip to Abo Rasheed's workshop rectified the problem, and summer went on as it had for centuries, with youth swimming, diving and fishing off the coast of Beirut, the ancient city by the sea.

20th century seismic shifts

The 20th century saw many drastic political seismic shifts take place in the Middle East. At the end of the First World War, the fall of the Ottoman Empire led to a redrawing of the map of the Middle East by the victorious allies, under the auspices of the League of Nations. Britain was to run the affairs of Palestine, while France did so in Lebanon.

France had a history of close relations with the Lebanese Christian Maronites. The French Jesuit missionaries had established two schools there in 1770, and in 1875 they opened Saint Joseph University in Beirut. French influence grew considerably after the war as they established a very effective health, education and judiciary system.

In 1943, Lebanon was given its independence from France and became the modern democracy it is today, with a multireligious tapestry. The new constitution divided power along religious lines; the president would be a Christian Maronite, the prime minister a Sunni Muslim, and the speaker of the house a Shia Muslim. That decision unfortunately introduced sectarianism into the constitution, a flaw that ensured constant tension between old-world loyalty to one's religion and clan and loyalty to the new democratic constitution of this ancient land. Be that as it may, the leaders of all the religions represented in Lebanon agreed to work together as they embarked on a new golden age of peace and prosperity.

Meanwhile, in neighboring Palestine, the British played a double game. In 1917, British Foreign Secretary Arthur James Balfour wrote a letter to Baron Rothchild, a wealthy and prominent leader in the Jewish community, expressing the British government's support for the establishment of a Jewish home in Palestine. This letter was published in the press and became known as the Balfour Declaration.

The League of Nations in 1923 gave Great Britain the responsibility of establishing a Jewish national homeland in British-controlled Palestine. After the end of the Second World War a massive and well-organized influx of European Jewish Zionists flooded Palestine. In 1948 the modern state of Israel was established. The jubilant creation of Israel by the European Zionists took place at the expense of the catastrophic uprooting of the native Palestinians who up until then lived in peace with the native Jews who never left for Europe. The Palestinians were kicked out of their homes, villages, towns and cities that they had lived in for centuries.

Entire villages were systematically demolished, with numerous massacres perpetrated by the newly arriving Europeans, the details of which are documented by, among others, the renowned Jewish scholar and Israeli historian and professor Ilan Pappe in his book *The Ethnic Cleansing of Palestine*.

It is said that one of the marks of an established and advanced civilization is its ability to acknowledge its historical transgressions, injustices and the crimes of its past. Ilan Pappe's book was such an effort. Albeit ahead of its time, as Israel for decades has continued its evictions and demolitions of Palestinian homes and villages while funding settlement expansion and the occupation and suppression of the Palestinians.

One of the tragic ironies of history is that European Jews fleeing persecution and antisemitism by Europeans would, in creating their new state of Israel, kill and displace a people who had nothing to do with how they were treated in Europe, culminating in the horrible atrocities of the Holocaust during the Second World War. It was another example of how often in history the oppressed become oppressors. More than 400,000 Palestinian refugees fled north to Lebanon, with an equal number fleeing east to Jordan. The refugee camps in both host countries were densely packed.

The larger and wealthier Arab states of Egypt, Iraq, Syria, Saudi Arabia and the Gulf states began funding and arming the newly formed Palestine Liberation Organization (PLO), with the intention of creating a Palestinian military organization that would regain the Palestinian homeland for its people. The refugee camps were flooded with weapons and began transforming from refugee camps administered by international relief agencies into armed fortresses organized and controlled by the PLO.

While the Muslim leaders in Lebanon allied themselves with the plight and cause of the Palestinians' armed struggle, the Lebanese Christian Maronite Nationalists, while initially sympathetic and welcoming to the Palestinian refugees, grew more skeptical and alarmed at the militarization of the Palestinian refugee camps.

The Nationalists had serious cause for concern after seeing the PLO try to overthrow the government of another host country, Jordan. The Jordanians fought off the PLO's attempt to take control of their country and won their war of sovereignty, expelling the PLO from Jordan and landing them in Lebanon, on top of an already loaded deck, and adding fuel to what was becoming a combustible situation.

As the Arab countries continued to pour more money and weapons into the coffers of the PLO, the organization grew in strength and developed an army that rivaled that of the host country, Lebanon. The PLO also grew in flagrant abuse of its power and began to expand its sphere of influence by dictating political events in Lebanon to the point where the Lebanese army was not allowed into parts of its own country, parts controlled by the PLO. The PLO in effect had become its own state within the state of Lebanon.

In response, the Lebanese Christian Nationalists ramped up the arming and training of their militias and began conducting organized, disciplined military training camps in the mountains. The number of enlisted soldiers in the Nationalist militias was outnumbered four to one by the PLO's forces. The difference in weapons and ammunition was even greater.

The Nationalists made up the difference with many young, motivated volunteers who came up the ranks of the Boy Scout summer programs. Most were between the ages of 15 and 18. Also, volunteering was a cross-section of the population: teachers, students, shopkeepers, office workers, farmers, fishermen, construction workers, barbers and butchers.

The largest and most organized of the Nationalist militias was Pierre Gemayel's Phalange Kataeb Party. Allied with the Phalange were the Chamoun Tigers of Freedom, the Tanzeem, and the Guardians of The Cedars, along with volunteers sympathetic to their common cause. The militia buildup and daily rhetoric were omens of the dark days ahead.

Prelude to a civil war

Most Lebanese barely noticed the beginnings of a civil war brewing as they went on with their daily lives. Dimitri continued to go to school, help his younger cousins with their homework, and work at his uncle's shop, delivering propane tanks in the neighborhood. His older cousin Jabril was active in the Phalange militia and would return from the latest skirmish with the PLO with dark and cautionary tales of the inevitability of war. The skirmishes and clashes were at first limited to rival neighborhoods, like Chiyah and Ein El Remmaneh. Sin El Feil, Dekwaneh and Tel El Zatar all had a marked increase in confrontations between the Christian Nationalists and the PLO.

Muslim political parties, having felt underrepresented by the constitution that favored the Maronite Christians, decided to ally themselves with the PLO, not only in support of the Palestinian cause, but also seeing in the alliance a chance to shift more power in their favor. The politicians and warlords would manage to rein in their fighters and quell the violence, keeping the illusion of normalcy within reach. They called these incidents and flareups "The Troubles" (*al hawadess,*) a minimizing term that suggested a solution was still close at hand.

For a long time, life in the rest of Beirut continued as if nothing unusual was happening. People went on with their lives, simply avoiding the dangerous neighborhoods. The hotels, restaurants and nightclubs were still full of tourists and the beaches packed with sunbathers. During this surreal period, people fought in the streets wearing masks and hoods to avoid being recognized by a friend, acquaintance or enemy with whom they might have to share a place of work, office or a classroom. Instead of the Lebanese army boldly and decisively putting a stop to the violence, it was given orders to remain in its barracks, in the fear that it might split along sectarian lines.

Dimitri's neighborhood was among others not far from the seaport and the Phalange headquarters of Seifi. The residents of the neighborhood were constantly on edge, watching for unusual vehicles and unfamiliar faces that might be casing the headquarters.

But life continued, despite the new level of tension. Schools remained in session, couples married, and children were born. On one of these "normal" days, a loud explosion rang out in the neighborhood.

Teta let out a scream *"Ya dillee! Ya dillee!"* Dimitri stopped doing his homework on the living room table and ran out to the balcony. He saw his neighbor Jocelyne Khoueiry carrying a rifle and running out of her building and up the street, following her brothers, who were likewise armed and running towards the explosion.

At 19, Jocelyne was three years older than Dimitri, who admired her and had a teenage crush on her. All the younger kids in the neighborhood loved her and looked up to her as an older sister. She had watched over and tutored many of them. Jocelyne had a degree of empathy, maturity and sense of responsibility beyond her years. She was naturally maternal to the neighborhood kids and equally at ease in conversations with adults and senior citizens, who saw her as a ray of sunshine in their daily lives.

Jocelyne was not absorbed by the usual teenage angst, whims, fancy and fantasy most girls her age were immersed in. She was fully engaged in life and was very present and in the moment, always helping someone, sensitively listening or cheerfully joking. Volleyball was her passion, and she was often seen walking to and from school with books under one arm and a volleyball under the other. Jocelyne could outrun, outswim, outdive and outfish most boys, yet had a sense of modesty and a sweet smile that made it look like she was amused by it all. The only ones more amused than she herself were the older women of the neighborhood, who saw her as a trailblazer. Even when Jocelyne was a child, Teta used to say, "That girl is an old spirit visiting this earth. May God protect her."

She had grown up in a typical middle-class Lebanese Maronite home with older brothers who were members of Gemayel's Nationalist Phalange Kataeb Party. Her brother Fadi was admired by all the boys in the neighborhood for his athleticism and gregarious good nature.

A half-hour after the explosion, Jocelyne returned to her building with her brothers. Teta called out from the balcony to the street below: "*Shoo ya Fadi? Kheir inshalla?*" (What is it Fadi? Good, God willing?). Fadi responded, "*Baseeta ya Taunte*, it was only a propane tank that exploded. It had a faulty relief valve."

The hammer drops

On April 13, 1975, in the neighborhood of Ain El Remmaneh, Pierre Gemayel was the guest of honor at the opening of a new church, named Our Lady of Salvation. It was a highly festive occasion, and people turned out in droves. Gemayel, who was loved and revered by his people, came out of the church to the delight of a cheering crowd gathered on the sidewalks and the balconies and rooftops of neighborhood buildings. As Gemayel waved to the crowd, a car appeared, moving at high speed with armed men inside opening fire at the church, missing Pierre Gemayel, but killing one of his bodyguards. Immediately, Gemayel was protected and whisked away to safety.

What remained were armed men from the neighborhood, on edge and seething with anger at what had just taken place. Shortly thereafter, a bus with 27 Palestinians aboard, returning from an event held at Tel El Zatar, turned into the street where the attempted assassination of Pierre Gemayel took place. The passengers on the bus were singing songs and chanting Palestinian revolutionary slogans, unaware of what had happened on the street they were entering. As the bus made its way down the street, some say its engine backfired, others that they heard gunshots. Either way, it was enough to trigger the edgy residents to unleash a barrage of gunfire at the bus from the rooftops above, killing all 27 people on board. When the deafening sound of gunfire subsided, the bus rolled silently down the street and came to a quiet standstill at a gasoline station.

At that moment the Lebanese civil war was ignited. The Lebanese Nationalists and the PLO fought gun battles in the streets, alleys and across the rooftops of buildings in the densely populated city.

*   *   *

Avenues, streets, and alleys leading to the various rival neighborhoods were soon blocked, and city blocks were made into makeshift fortresses guarded on both sides with sandbags, gravel-filled barrels, cars, trucks, city municipal buses and shipping containers from the nearby seaport. Heavily armed men and teenagers fought each other across the barricades with machine guns and rocket-propelled grenades.

The tensions and skirmishes that had preceded this day gave way to full-scale urban street warfare that spread quickly across the city. The Nationalist Phalange Militia put out the call for volunteers to turn out and help secure the fluid, ever shifting front line along a six-kilometer stretch. Allied with the Phalange militia were the Guardians of The Cedars, the Tanzeem and the Tigers of Freedom militias. Hundreds of posts were filled by teenagers managed by captains not much older than they were, most in their early to mid-twenties. The Bejin commandos of the Phalange would make the rounds, dropping off ammunition and offering tactical advice and support, before moving on to the next post to strengthen it.

Downtown Beirut, and Martyrs' Square in particular, became the epicenter of the most intense and contested battles. The iconic bronze statue, a national symbol for a golden age, representing hope and a bright future, became riddled with bullets fired from both sides of the conflict.

The PLO and their allies were inflicting high casualties on the Phalange posts from the 35-story Mur Tower, a partially built skyscraper that became a sniper's nest overlooking the neighborhoods of east Beirut.

In the early fall of 1975, the Christian Nationalist militias, led by the Phalange, were united as they moved to take control of the hotel district, with the Phalange Bejin Commandos taking over the 26-story Holiday Inn. By doing so, they flanked the Mur Tower and established their own machine-gun posts and sniper nests overlooking the Kantari neighborhood controlled by the PLO and their allies.

The Nationalists took over the Saint George, Phoenicia, Hilton and Normandy hotels, in what became known as the hotel wars. Fighting was fierce and at very close range, often culminating in hand-to-hand combat through hallways and from room to room. The hotels changed hands several times before the Phalange managed to establish control of the hotel district in late fall, before winter set in.

* * *

A few months into the civil war, the old lives and daily routines of the city's golden age had faded into a distant memory. And in its place a new, all-consuming reality of unpredictability set in, as mortars, rockets and gunfire rained on the neighborhoods all along the front lines. Dimitri and his cousin Jabril became regular volunteers with the Phalange. Many of their Boy Scout friends from summer camp were with them as well.

Teta and Samira pleaded with Dimitri and his cousins to stay away from the downtown and hotel district front lines and leave the fighting to the legitimate Lebanese Army, while they helped the community with much-needed civic action instead.

Dimitri's uncle Ramzi had worked for the municipality all his adult life and believed in the legitimacy of government institutions. He believed the legitimate Lebanese Army was the protector of the country's constitution and rule of law. "Don't do anything hasty!" he would say. "The Lebanese army is going to put a stop to this madness."

But Dimitri, Jabril and many of their friends believed that was no longer possible, as the army had been relegated to its barracks by the country's politicians for fear it might split along sectarian lines.

So, the pleas of Teta and Samira fell on deaf ears. The well indoctrinated teenagers were stubborn, rebellious, and driven by youthful absolutism and delusions of their own invincibility. National fervor was at an all-time high. And with the death of one of Dimitri and Jabril's core friends, the die was cast. There would be no turning back.

* * *

While the battles in the streets and alleys raged on, downtown Beirut was turning into a surreal labyrinth of destroyed, empty, desolate, haunted buildings. Walking through on patrols in the buildings along the "Green Line" that divided Martyrs' Square, Dimitri was struck by the drastic change from just a year ago, when he and his friends had joyfully ventured into the fish market to buy a fish trap from Abo Rasheed's workshop. He remembered how the area was bustling with life and activity. Now, the fish market, Abo Rasheed's workshop and the shops and souks were all destroyed. The whole downtown that had been the heart and vibrant pulse of the city for centuries was now left to the haunting winds, a mere echo of its illustrious past.

A six-kilometer stretch of the metropolis divided the city into east Beirut and west Beirut. The Green Line, as it came to be known, was a no-man's land between the warring sides. It was heavily mined and watched over by snipers on both sides, who shot at anyone and anything that moved across the line.

On the west side of Waygand Street, in what had been the coffee market, there was a partially built building that the PLO was able to control during the day to harass a Phalange post down the street, one of a series of posts defending the Beirut port. The post was being defended by none other than Dimitri's neighbor, Jocelyne who was now in command of an all-women's division of the Phalange militia known as the Bajinat. Jocelyne noticed that the PLO withdrew from the vulnerable building every evening before sunset and headed back to their fortifications on the other side of Waygand Street and into their stronghold of the Kantari neighborhood. After days of surveillance, Jocelyne and her all-female troop drafted a plan to move into the building under the cover of darkness. The highly trained women commandos moved in unison, like ghosts riding on a night fog, as they passed through the alleys and corridors leading to the building. Six of the women secured the entrances, while Jocelyne and seven others went upstairs and moved the sniper nest's sandbags from the back of the building that was facing the port to the opposite side facing Waygand Street. Then they waited for dawn.

The next morning, PLO soldiers started to make their way to the building, crossing Waygand Street and filtering through the alleys leading to the building Jocelyne and her crew were holding. When they got to the building, they were caught by surprise and met with a hail of bullets; forcing them to withdraw back to their fortifications in the Kantari neighborhood.

A story was published in the press describing how a group of 13 young women led by Jocelyne Khoueiry took over the building and, by doing so, managed to push the Phalange front line two blocks forward. The newspaper article must have stirred the prideful ire of the PLO commander who had lost the building to the daring women.

He decided to wage an all-out offensive to retake the building with overwhelming force. PLO fighters, in a hastily contrived, half-baked plan, moved towards the building. The Phalange women defenders were well positioned and entrenched to offer fierce resistance. As gun battles raged between the building and the street and alleys of the coffee market, Jocelyne ran up the steps with a string of hand grenades, and with a Hail Mary lobbed one from the roof of the building to the street below, triggering a frenzy of commotion, confusion and disarray in the ranks of the invaders. In less than a minute, the PLO unexpectedly withdrew, and the guns fell silent while debris settled, and smoke dissipated.

The women guarding the building looked at each other, puzzled at this turn of events. As it turned out, Jocelyne's grenade had found its way to the commander of the invading force killing him instantly, creating chaos and confusion among his troops, who had picked up his body and quickly withdrew. Jocelyne Khoueiry became an iconic figure of the Lebanese Nationalist resistance.

The war continued to grind on, and the Green Line became a forest thick with weeds and trees growing in the exposed dirt of the once-paved streets that were now scarred from heavy mortar fire. The soil beneath the asphalt had been liberated for nature to once again take over. The cityscape had an eerie surreal appearance now, conjuring up an apocalyptic vision of what metropolitan cities would look like if humanity were suddenly to vanish, leaving nature to reclaim the earth that was once covered and paved by progress.

The Green Line

All along the Green Line, posts became permanent and fortified. The war was beginning to settle into something that resembled the trench warfare of the First World War. But instead of trenches, there were city blocks of buildings facing each other.

During the first year of the civil war, in areas far behind the Green Line, life went on in the divided city. Couples married, kids attended school, and families went to the market for their daily needs, with ever-growing shortages filled by a thriving black market of enterprising entrepreneurs, some altruistic, some greedy opportunists, and some criminal.

The fighting remained confined to the front lines along the Green Line, with the most intense and volatile battles taking place in downtown Beirut and the hotel district. That's the area where the center of commerce, banks, parliament and the city port were located. Controlling that sector of the city was to control the lifeline of the country.

For Dimitri, Jabril, Elie, George, Jocelyne and her brothers, and many others living in the world of Sector 4 in Beirut's downtown and the hotel district, life became a surreal existence of extreme contrasts. At home, not too far from the front line, Dimitri lived a relatively normal domesticated existence, helping his younger cousins with their homework, stocking his uncle's store, and delivering propane tanks to the buildings in the neighborhood.

When it was time for Dimitri and Jabril's shift to start along the Green Line, their fellow Phalange militiamen would pull up at the building in their cars and the cousins would load up and head to the Phalange Seifi headquarters, parking the cars in a nearby underground garage. Once briefed and prepared, they would line up and load into a column of M113 armored personnel carriers like sardines in a ten-ton can on iron tracks sitting in two rows facing each other. The M113 column of personnel carriers would fire up their diesel engines and head out, rumbling along on their track chains while billowing thick diesel exhaust in their wake.

When the armored carrier reached the front line, the driver would back up to the building's lobby. The doors would swing open and Dimitri, Jabril and the rest of the troop would spill out into the building they would be defending and patrolling for the next 72 hours. After the captains exchanged information on the latest moves and positions of the enemy, the relieved and exhausted shift would load up into the M113s for the return to headquarters, and from there to their cars in the underground garage that would take them home for much-needed rest.

At last, a new ceasefire and peace initiative was being worked out. All was quiet on the hotel front as the Phalange continued to keep a vigil on the streets below the Holiday Inn. The teenagers on break stretched, exercised, and ran sprints in the hallways. They even played football with a makeshift ball made of rolled-up bed linens and tape. The older militiamen brewed coffee and smoked cigarettes.

Raymon was a child prodigy pianist before the war and a star pupil at the Salibi Music School of Beirut.

During breaks from guard duty, he would warm up on the hotel's grand piano with the Lebanese national anthem, lifting everyone's spirits and morale, followed by the Phalange anthem, and Sharbil joining in with a *darbuka* drum left behind by the musicians who had been performing for a wedding at the hotel when it was stormed by the Phalange. Sharbil would drum with gusto while everyone stomped their feet in unison as they sang the Phalange anthem and its repetitive refrain of *"Kataeb."*

Machine-gun fire from the buildings across the Holiday Inn would put a rude stop to the boisterous anthem. Profanities would be exchanged before Dimitri, Jabril and the rest of the hotel guards would respond with fire of their own. The Holiday Inn Phalange guards had to conserve their ammunition with a response that was short, yet intense. It was nothing serious, just a way to tell each other that they were there, aware of each other and ready.

After the intense exchange of gunfire going out and coming in through the balconies and windows of the Holiday Inn, the deafening sound of the exchange, along with the projectiles and debris bouncing off the concrete hotel room walls would be followed by a numbed silence and then a persistent ringing in the ears. The smell of gunpowder mixed with the cold, misty sea breeze of winter was thick and palpable.

"That was a close one, cousin, I swear you are a cat with nine lives." Jabril said to Dimitri.

"It's OK, that means I have three more left," Dimitri responded laughing in the face of death before the adrenaline subsided. The mood then turned serious, and both crossed themselves while saying a prayer for their fallen brothers in arms and thanking their guardian angels.

As the day passed, the sun began its descent into the deep blue sea while the sky took on the dark, steely gray sunset of winter, so different from the warm orange glow of summer and the joyful memories of summers past. Raymon sat behind the hotel's grand piano and broke the silence with "Trois Gymnopedies" by French composer Erik Satie. These were haunting compositions, with long spans between the key notes that resonated with the soul and traveled through the empty hallways and corridors of the hotel, strewn with glass and debris from previous battles.

The militiamen were transfixed and transported by the melancholy melody delivered by Raymon, who, unbeknown to them, was a sensitive and talented musician. The music resonated with their deeper feelings about the state of things. A few hushed minutes followed the final note as it faded away.

Then, as if a switch had been triggered, Captain Elie instantly resumed his upbeat posture and confident persona. "*Yala ya shabab*. Let's get ready for the new shift." Everyone shook off their emotions and returned to their vigilant state of mind and the task at hand.

On this cold and damp winter night, thirty Phalange militiamen appeared from the adjoining alleys under cover of darkness to relieve the exhausted guards at the end of their three-day stay at the Holiday Inn. Food had been plentiful at the hotel during the first few weeks of fighting, but it had long since run out and the water had been cut off. The new shifts had to pack their own food and water, along with their weapons and ammunition. Their backpacks were heavy and cumbersome, especially when they had to crawl through exposed areas strewn with concrete and steel from the blown-out buildings leading to the hotel.

When the new shift arrived at the Holiday Inn, Captain Elie briefed Captain Fadi on the past three days' events. Fadi in return pointed out the safe route of return and any dangerous and vulnerable intersections that should be avoided by the returning militiamen on their way back to headquarters.

"Be careful crossing Salloum Street. There was a sniper there when we were on our way here. We are sending a team to neutralize him. It should be taken care of by the time you get there. But be careful; it's a vulnerable intersection." Elie thanked Fadi as everyone prepared for the crossing back to headquarters and then home.

In the first few months of the civil war, Sector 4 was a volatile area, with buildings and whole blocks changing hands, keeping the front-line fluid. Dimitri, Jabril and the rest of their troop, led by Elie, headed back to headquarters under the cover of darkness along Jbail Street, making their way through a labyrinthine complex of alleys and emerging onto Agrippa Street, heading towards the sea before turning right onto Riskallah Street and into a building that took them to the vulnerable and dangerous Salloum Street crossing. After crossing Salloum, taking turns giving each other cover, they arrived at a building that had dozens of holes sledge-hammered through the concrete block walls; this led the Phalange into the Normandy Hotel, where they could feel relatively safe, knowing that the worst danger was over.

From the gathering point at the Normandy Hotel's large, rounded lobby facing the sea, the Phalange troop loaded into a column of M113 armored personnel carriers lined up at what used to be the taxi drop-off point for hotel guests. Palm trees and ornate Parisian streetlights still lined both sides of the sea front road that, not long ago, had been a favorite destination for tourists. The M113s then took the Phalange militiamen to the headquarters at Seifi. From there, they walked to a nearby building and down a concrete driveway to their cars in the underground garage. At last, they made it back to their neighborhoods and homes for much-needed rest.

The horror

With a new peace initiative underway, the fighting downtown subsided and became limited to minor clashes between undisciplined elements, which were quickly reined in. After the carnage and destruction of the past few months, everyone was hopeful that a solution was at hand.

It was in this atmosphere that Roland and three of his friends, all members of the Phalange, decided to go to the movies, something that had been impossible during the past few dark months. Roland's father, Joseph, was a senior member of the Phalange militia, a charismatic and jovial character affectionately called "Uncle Joseph" by all the young Phalange members who grew up with his sons. Uncle Joseph had suffered a tragedy in July involving his son Elie, Roland's younger brother. Elie had been on his way to the International Rally Race, which started in Beirut, passed over two mountain ranges and ended in the Syrian desert. Along the way, Elie and two friends were ambushed and killed.

The family was still in mourning, yet Joseph was happy to see his surviving son, Roland, starting to lighten up and joke again with his friends. There was hope on the street as well. The guns remained silent, and the negotiations continued. People on all sides longed for a return to normalcy and rebuilding.

Roland and his friends headed out to the movies on a Friday night, December 5, 1975. Saturday morning, Roland's family awoke to find Roland had not returned. Joseph called his son's friends and their families and learned they had not returned home either after the movie outing. Joseph rushed down to the Phalange headquarters at Seifi, where armed men had begun to gather, more pouring into headquarters as the news spread. The building was filling up with heavily armed men anxiously awaiting news on the whereabouts of Roland and his friends.

Joseph sat behind a table with three telephones, reaching out to the various politicians and warlords, asking for any information on the young men's whereabouts, pleading with them to intervene and bring his son Roland and his friends home safely. An hour passed before a report came into headquarters that the young men had been kidnapped and were being held at the heavily armed Tel El Zaatar camp by the PLO.

In a state of hysteria, Uncle Joseph came up with a spontaneous plan to gather hostages who could be exchanged for their release.

"*Yalla ya shabab*, follow me!" he called out as he headed out of the Phalange's Seifi headquarters and carried on to Charles Helou Avenue, across from the Beirut port, where dozens of Phalange militiamen set up roadblocks. Unsuspecting traffic drove into the Phalange's snare and came to a complete stop while the militiamen checked the ID cards of the car's occupants.

ID cards in Lebanon have the standard picture and pertinent information, along with information about the card-holder's religion. Christians, women and children were allowed to pass through the roadblocks and leave, while Palestinian and Muslim men were escorted at gunpoint to a nearby building. After two hours, more than 150 innocent civilian men sat crouched next to each other in a dark, damp and cold underground garage, bewildered, confused and terrified.

* * *

An hour passed before a confirmed eyewitness report came into Phalange headquarters stating that the bodies of four young men had been found on the side of the road near Tel El Zaatar. The bodies were riddled with bullets and finished with hatchet blows to the head. It was Roland and his friends. The recipient of the grim news ran down to Charles Helou Avenue to tell Joseph and his men the tragic news.

It was reported that Joseph, who had been in a manic state, yelling out orders while gathering hostages, was transformed into a silent entity of darkness. The yelling, screaming and ordering stopped. He and a group of armed men headed to the underground garage where the hostages were being held. There would be no survivors.

The killing went on above ground as well. Palestinian and Muslim men were rounded up at the checkpoints and shot point-blank, their bodies dragged, then stacked in high piles on street corners of an intersection in a gruesome display of depravity and madness. The carnage continued unabated, ignoring telephone and relayed orders to stop. It took the commander of the Phalange, William Hawi, to show up on the scene and intervene in person to finally put a stop to it.

At noon the guns fell silent, leaving more than 400 innocent civilian men dead. Men who were fathers, sons and brothers, whose place of birth and religion as they appeared on their identification cards was the only reason, they would not be returning home.

Dimitri and Jabril were home when they heard the gruesome news. It was shocking and deeply saddening. They had signed up to defend their community against the PLO, but this was something quite different. They had grown up with Muslim friends at school and on the football field, where the camaraderie was brotherly. Before the tensions that led up to the civil war, no one ever asked or cared what the other's religion was.

The event became known as Black Saturday. To Dimitri, it was a turning point and a twisted betrayal.

The tragic psychotic break experienced by one person in a position of authority had caused the mindless death of more than 400 innocent people and guaranteed the same fate for countless others, by ushering in a new wave of retaliatory madness. War that had started with each side believing in their just and noble cause had instantly morphed into mindless, endless carnage. The foolishness and depravity of war had entered a new dimension.

The PLO and their Muslim allies predictably retaliated by setting up their own floating roadblocks and executing those caught with the wrong ID papers in the wrong neighborhood at the wrong time.

In protest, the bravest people in the country took to the streets. Lebanese Muslims, Christians, Druze and Jews all walked hand in hand, chanting "No to sectarianism! Yes, to peace and reconciliation! We are all brothers and sisters!" They put action to their words by publicly scratching out the religious denomination from their ID cards.

While most of the population shared in these sentiments and beliefs, the war Jinn was out of the bottle and could not be put back in. The Afreet, having clasped its hand with the country in its grip, ensured that this dark chapter in the ancient city's history had to play itself out.

The horrific tragedy of Black Saturday marked a turning point in the civil war. It opened the gates of hell wide open and changed something in the collective psyche of all Lebanese. The somber realization set in that the country had taken a decisive and unretractable step into the abyss.

*　　*　　*

Days, weeks and months passed as the dysfunction and horror of the civil war became routine. People kept score of the dead, casualties and losses, searching through the lengthening lists of names published in the newspapers with anxious curiosity to see if a relative, friend or acquaintance appeared among them.

As the war ground on, there ceased to be a functioning central government. It existed only in name. Everyone belonged and relied on their warlord and militia. Chaos ruled as law and order broke down.

New, heavily armed renegade gangs loosely affiliated with the various militias roamed the streets, setting up roadblocks. These renegade groups had nothing to do with the original cause of either side. They were criminals, in it for the money. They dealt in smuggling weapons, contraband, kidnapping and ransom. They even hired foreign professional thieves from Europe to crack open the safes in the banking district while under their protection, the most prized being the British Royal Bank of the Middle East. All the bank's safes and safe deposit boxes were completely emptied.

Dimitri and Jabril remained loyal volunteers, answering directly and only to headquarters for assignments. They remained committed to the cause, even though they were seeing it erode and were starting to question where all this was going. A commitment to what they believed to be a patriotic and honorable cause was being replaced by massacres and thievery.

Money and weapons poured into the coffers of all sides of the conflict. The war that started with street skirmishes between the Christian Nationalists and the PLO had transformed into a sectarian religious war. Then it morphed even further into a regional and international proxy war, fought on Lebanese soil.

It was the height of the Cold War, which turned hot in various regions of the world and in Beirut in particular. It was a conflict fought among the world powers through their proxies, on a chessboard consisting of the little country of Lebanon. Events on the ground seemed to be controlled by a puppet master, who was in turn controlled by a higher puppet master.

Mercenaries, missionaries
and misfits

The Lebanese civil war became a magnet for all sorts of unlikely characters and organizations. The trifecta of mercenaries, missionaries and misfits poured into the country.

The Japanese Red Army and other communist organizations joined the fight alongside the PLO and their allies. The Phalange Christian Nationalists also attracted freelancers. French mercenary Dominique Borella was fighting the Khmer Rouge in Cambodia when the civil war in Lebanon broke out. He and his men were the last holdouts defending the Pochentong Airport from the advancing Khmer Rouge, who were interested in taking the airport intact and in return negotiated safe passage for Dominique and his men. He was evacuated to Thailand before heading to Lebanon to advise and fight with the Phalange and secure Beirut's port, the country's lifeline.

Dimitri and Jabril admired Dominique for his knowledge and ability to foresee all potential threats while drafting an ironclad plan to defend an area. His reputation had preceded him, and upon meeting him Dimitri understood why. Dominique had a brilliant strategic and tactical mind.

He designed multi layered defenses that had a track record of defeating invaders with a much larger army. He also had charisma and a knack for bringing everyone on board, inspiring them to be as committed to a plan as he is. He was admired for his extensive track record, which began in 1955 when, as an 18-year-old French soldier, he became one of the youngest recipients of the Medaille Militaire. Twenty years later, he was in Beirut advising the Phalange.

Dominique was a larger-than-life character who seemed to be touched by a special spirit. In the ancient world, they would have attributed this quality to the dark gods of war. His comrades and allies saw him as a heroic savior and gallant warrior. Others, while happy to have him on their side, thought he was odd and a bit delusional, especially when he was partaking in a glass of cognac and a cigar and talking about being a reincarnated Crusader who had been in Lebanon centuries before and had come back to life to fulfill his timeless duty.

And then there were his enemies, who saw him simply as an opportunistic, crafty and ruthless demon of war. Whatever he was, he certainly was an extraordinary and unusual character.

In September 1975, Dominique Borella was killed in combat in downtown Beirut. He was felled in front of the Rivoli Theater in Martyrs' Square by a PLO sniper's bullet. Borella's plan had called on the Phalange to push their defensive lines further into the city and away from the port, to allow for the building of heavy fortifications around the port.

The Phalange embarked on this costly mission by pushing their line of defense to include the buildings on the west side of Martyrs' Square, up from the sea towards Waygand Street and leading all the way to the hotel district. Battles raged on the new front lines, with a spike in Phalange casualties as they came out of their well-held defensive positions and embarked on a costly offensive. The mission allowed engineers and builders to move in heavy machinery and build the port's formidable defenses without being constantly subjected to snipers.

Months later, in an attempt to break through the heavy fortifications, the PLO and their allies embarked on a campaign to enlist mercenaries for use as cannon fodder for a major attack on the port.

Libya's Muammar Gaddafi sent advisors, along with millions of dollars, to the PLO. The money was spent on weapons and recruiting hundreds of mercenaries from the impoverished countryside of Somalia. The pitch to the Somali mercenaries was a combination of monetary reward and religious zealotry, the same age-old combination that is often irresistible to lost, young, unemployed men experiencing economic and social hardships.

There was no shortage of young men in the prime of their lives who enthusiastically signed up for the mission. After crossing the Gulf of Aden, the Somali mercenaries were packed on trucks like oblivious cattle headed to the slaughterhouse. The capacity of man to exploit others is as old as history, and this was yet another tragic chapter of many.

When the truckloads of Somali mercenaries arrived in Lebanon, they were fed and housed in tents for a week of training. On the day of the offensive, they were given no helmets or flak jackets, but did receive plenty of stimulants before being ordered to storm the Phalange defenses.

Borella's defensive blueprint and the tenacious resistance of the Phalange held up against the waves of Somali mercenaries, who were repelled with heavy machine-gun fire. The carnage was extensive. A few of the Somalis, who were amped up and wired beyond natural life, made it close enough to the Phalange defenses to lob their grenades before collapsing. But most did not make it past the start of the charge. Borella's defensive plan held up and secured the port.

After that major battle, there was another lull in the fighting as the politicians returned to the negotiating table. Dimitri and his troop arrived one day to relieve the previous shift defending a row of buildings leading to the Phoenicia Hotel. Walking into the lobby of the building, he saw his old friend Paul from Boy Scout days. Seeing Paul felt like seeing a bright light amid the war's darkness. The two old friends greeted each other and caught up briefly, each instructing the other to relay their love and best wishes to each other's families.

The thick diesel smoke from the M113s' idling engines was a welcome smell that covered the stench of rotting flesh, feces and urine permeating the air around the heavily fought for buildings that Dimitri and his comrades were preparing to defend for the next 72 hours. Before leaving, Paul had told Dimitri that their Boy Scout captain, Maron, was on the fifth floor of the building, in command of a notorious group of rogue militiamen that had posted themselves there and had made a row of buildings on the front lines their de facto mini satellite headquarters. The gang of rogue militiamen ran a lucrative black market that smuggled in weapons and contraband.

Dimitri gave Paul a puzzled look. Paul shook his head in disappointment "He's not the captain Maron we knew from the Boy Scout days. The war has changed him a lot." Before Dimitri could ask more, Paul had to board the M113 for his trip back to headquarters. The two said their goodbyes and Dimitri, along with his fellow militiamen, were briefed and given their new posts to defend.

On his first break, Dimitri headed up the stairs to visit his old Scout captain. When he reached the fifth floor, the sentry at the top of the stairs recognized him from a shift they'd served together at the Holiday Inn a couple of months back. After mutual greetings Dimitri got the green light to head down the long hallway to see Captain Maron.

Along the way, he passed a row of men sitting in chairs behind sandbags that had been stacked up to the ceiling to cover the interior of the walls that faced the Green Line. The men looked eerily lifeless and were propped up by sandbags that looked like pillows holding their frames in a permanent position as they peered into their rifle scopes through small openings in the wall. Dimitri walked past them and turned the corner into a room protected by the adjoining building that was also occupied by Maron's men. The sentry at the far corner gave Dimitri the go-ahead and announced his approach to Captain Maron who was in a room playing cards, a walkie-talkie by his side blurting out the latest reports from adjoining city blocks and buildings where his men were positioned. Maron looked pleasantly surprised to see Dimitri.

"*Ahlan bil abaday!*" he called out. Dimitri came to attention with a stomp of his right heel and a salute to his old Boy Scout captain.

Before the war, Captain Maron had known how to motivate his Scouts. He dispensed nicknames and custom praises for each one. He made people feel special. He understood what made men tick on a very basic and primal level.

Captain Maron was both educated and street smart; he could inspire men from different backgrounds, and talked to people on their own level, engendering their trust by making them feel he was one of them, someone who understood them regardless of who they were or what social or economic background they came from. Captain Maron was as comfortable with a city slickster as he was with an earnest country boy or an intellectual scholar. He could be a best friend and a loyal ally, or a cold and ruthless enemy. He was a special kind of psychopath, one who before the war had seemed destined to become a great politician.

With the others at the card table, Maron shared some memorable and comical stories of the old camp days. "Too bad we don't have any walnuts for you to crack" said Maron laughing, as he told his men at the card table the story of how Dimitri used to crack walnuts with his bare hands around the campfire.

As the conversation shifted to more serious concerns about the enemy's activities in the buildings across the Green Line, one of Maron's men emerged from a hole that had been sledge-hammered through the wall of the adjoining building. Such passageways had been created through the walls of the adjacent four buildings, facilitating ease of movement from one building to another and forming a continuous line of defense along this stretch of the Green Line. The Phalange militiamen could easily navigate through the string of buildings to reinforce their positions where needed and counter the enemy's movements.

It was clear that the man approaching Maron was not well. He was weak and shivering, he looked like a dead man walking. He whispered something cryptic in what seemed like a desperate tone to Maron. Dimitri, feeling he was inadvertently intruding on a private conversation, excused himself and stepped out of the room walking down the hall to stand beside one of the motionless snipers. As he surveyed the scene, it became clear that Captain Maron was in command of a notorious group Dimitri had heard about on the street. The string of four buildings on the fifth floor was a den of drug addicts and hardened veterans with severe deficits in empathy, humanity and conscience.

They had started out as strong believers in the cause but had sunk to the point where the only thing that mattered to them was feeding their addiction. They would gladly man sniper nests for days, shooting anyone and anything that moved, as long as they were provided with their daily fix of uppers and downers. The troop of 40 killers had become an insular unit that functioned independently with Captain Maron at the helm. Heroin and cocaine were plentiful, since Maron supervised shipments of smuggled weapons and contraband. The higher-ups turned a blind eye because of the group's ruthless effectiveness and success on the urban battleground.

The sniper next to Dimitri took his eye off his rifle scope and looked up at him with a surprised expression, as if he had just realized that Dimitri was standing next to him. For hours on end, the sniper's whole world had been lived through his rifle scope and the small opening in the wall.

Puzzled, the sniper who seemed in a heroin fog, asked Dimitri, "How long have you been here?"

"I just got here with the new shift downstairs," he answered. "How about you?"

After a long pause, the ghost of a man answered sorrowfully, "I don't know. I really don't know." Then he returned his eye to his rifle saying, "You learn a lot about a man through a rifle scope."

Dimitri left the sniper to his lifeless pursuit. Leaving the disturbing scene, he walked past the row of sniper nests along the long corridor and headed towards the sentry who was manning the stairs. Just then, Captain Maron came out of his room and called out, "Don't be a stranger my friend. War is dirty, and everyone contributes to it in the way they can." Dimitri nodded silently, not in approval but in somber acceptance of a dark, cold fact. He then turned to the sentry and giving him a cynical smirk, said, "*Yaeesh Lubnan*" (Long live Lebanon) before heading down the steps, saddened and further disillusioned by what he had seen.

Dimitri and many others among the naïve boys of his youth looked up to Captain Maron before the war. But the man was no longer that person.

That night at his post, Dimitri had a lot of time to think. It was a turning point in how he saw the war and how he saw himself in it. He faced the grim realization that the ideals of the former boy scouts and choir boys who had once seen themselves as guardian angels fighting to defend their community and a righteous cause had given way to something much different; they had become demons of war.

In the heat of battle, the lines between good and evil were blurred. The concept itself had become meaningless. In these extreme states for survival, nature takes over and defines good as simply that which survives and bad as that which doesn't. When a group or a country's essential interests are involved, it uses any means it considers necessary to its survival. The ten commandments remain mute when self-preservation is at stake.

The fall of the Holiday Inn

Dimitri, Jabril, Paul, George, Elie, Samir and Fadi all had put in their time with 72-hour shifts at the Holiday Inn. It was considered an honor to be chosen to defend the hotel, which the Phalange referred to as "the castle." The building was at the farthest reaches of the front line. Luckily for them, on this day the old neighborhood friends were all elsewhere.

The PLO and their allies began to amass hundreds of fighters in the Kantari neighborhood. When the assembly was complete, heavy artillery and rocket fire began pounding the Holiday Inn and raining down on the streets that led to it. The intensity of the barrage and the bombardment of all accessible routes from downtown and the port made it clear that this was a prelude to something much bigger than just a normal exchange. It was preparation for an all-out offensive on the building.

The Phalange militiamen defending the hotel were isolated and on their own at that point. Reinforcements were held at bay with the continuous shelling and mortar fire at all connecting roads and pathways to the hotel. The first two assaults were repelled by the Phalange who were starting to run out of rocket-propelled grenades and ammunition. The third assault had an armored vehicle break through and ram its way past the first line of defense and into the Holiday Inn's lobby, creating a breach from which waves of PLO fighters and their allies started pouring into the building. The invading force took over and cleared the lobby while starting to make their way up the steps floor by floor, with battles raging between the defenders and invaders across the hotel's corridors and from room to room of each floor.

Finally, the assault reached the top floor, where the last of the Phalange militiamen were out of ammunition and surrounded. They were captured and thrown from the 24th story down to the street below. Their mangled bodies were defiled before being tied to car bumpers and dragged around the neighborhood surrounding the hotel in a sick celebration that left parts of disintegrating bodies strewn across the asphalt. The victors continued driving and dragging what little flesh remained on the fallen corpse.

The horrors of war and the revelation of what humans are capable of doing to each other could not have been imagined during the golden age of progress, peace and prosperity.

The elder statesmen who had ushered in that golden age with pragmatism and long-term vision handed over power to a younger generation, usually their sons, who grew up amid the tensions that led to the civil war. They were skeptical, edgy, reactionary, and far more ruthless than their predecessors.

The Nationalist militias went on a rampage and decided to eliminate all Palestinian presence in east Beirut. The Karantina massacre on January 18, 1976, took the lives of over a thousand Palestinians, triggering a response by the PLO and their allies two days later to invade the Christian town of Damour. Nineteen Phalange fighters defending the town and more than 500 civilians were massacred. Among the dead in Damour were the relatives of Elie Hubeika and his fiancé, the same Elie Hobeika who would, years later, command three companies of hardened veterans, including one particularly notorious company of psychopaths high out of their minds on cocaine, rage and revenge, in an attack on the Palestinian refugee camps of Sabra and Shatila, in what became one of the war's most grisly massacres.

*　　*　　*

The vicious cycle of violence was in full rotation and continued to turn and spin out of control. With each event there was further degradation of humanity, to the point that it degraded the collective soul of the nation. Nothing was surprising anymore. The golden age of Lebanon was long gone, relegated to the memory and nostalgia of a generation on its way to becoming part of the forgotten past. Another layer of this ancient city was turned to ruin, atop the remains of a brief but glorious era.

In 1976, the Syrian army was "invited" into Lebanon by the sitting president, in an effort to save his presidency and his people. The Syrian army entered under the guise of peacekeepers. It was like inviting a fox into a chicken yard to keep the roosters from killing each other. In time, the fox ate both roosters and all the chickens.

With the Syrians in control, the 1975-76 civil war came to a close. But the shifting political sands were heading towards an ominous future.

Dimitri, his friends and comrades were all affected in different ways. Some went underground and prepared for the inevitable next round. Others simply checked out, becoming disillusioned, lost and some even self-destructive. Others worked with their churches rebuilding their communities, while others migrated abroad to work and send money home to support their families and keep the economy from collapsing.

Dimitri remembered Saleem telling him while they had worked together during the summers before the war, "There will be times in life when you will be faced with having to make important decisions that will have a long-lasting effect on your future. When that time comes, don't indulgently take time off to think. Make sure to remain engaged in the moving river of life. Only then will the right decision and opportunity present itself. If you remain idle during this important time, you risk inviting trouble that will land you in the still waters and swamps of cynicism, doubt and darkness."

It's as if Saleem knew even before the war that difficult times lay ahead. Or maybe he simply understood the trials, tribulations and phases of life in general that everyone experiences and wanted to offer Dimitri directions for navigating safe passage towards a sound future.

Samira had continued to work during the war, researching the various editorials in the daily newspapers and writing reports on the events of the day from the perspective of varying and opposing views in the press. Her professor from her days at the American University of Beirut, Professor Jim Scott, and his wife, Susan, had become part of Samira's extended family over the years. They had moved back to the United States a few years before the war but remained in touch with Samira. They heard firsthand from her about the horrors of war and her sleepless nights of worry while her son was on guard duty downtown. In their latest letter to her, the Scotts offered to sponsor Dimitri, whom they had known from his birth to the age of 10, when they had left Lebanon.

It was a letter Samira received with great joy and trepidation. While the offer represented the opportunity of a lifetime for Dimitri, it also meant that she would not see her only son for at least five years.

America at the end of the Second World War, was seen by the world as the promised land, one founded on lofty ideals for the advancement of humanity. These ideals were not without contradictions, obstacles and setbacks, yet the dreamers and believers kept their eyes on the prize through it all.

Dimitri had grown up with American movies and based his perceptions about the United States on a teenage fantasy of what life would be like there. Samira had a more mature and seasoned outlook. She believed in democracy, freedom, liberty, human rights and a host of other enlightened and evolved views and causes that the United States ostensibly stood for.

Some in her family considered this naive. Uncle Emile, the conservative and pragmatic historian in the family, saw the United States as simply another great empire, like all the others that have come and gone. To him the United States was a new version of an old system that had at its core the same greed and expansionist goals as all the others. His critique was not biased or unreasonably directed towards America. He simply saw it as a negative trait of the human condition throughout history, with America being no different in that regard.

He saw the new empire of the 20th century laced with lip service to a higher moral code while offering financial snares of debt, consumerism and mindless entertainment that kept the population busy with upward mobility, busy with consumerism and consumption, as each person fulfilled his and her role as a cog in the gears of the new industrial empire, churning out products and weaponry and accumulating record corporate profits. Meanwhile, the new empire expanded its influence internationally and kept competitors in check with more than 700 military bases in 80 countries around the world.

Samira could not deny these facts, yet she saw things differently. Emile, she thought, had a limited and cynical perspective. She had faith in an evolving, fluid future where the possibilities were endless. She believed that with freedom, knowledge and courage, change for the better was possible and that America was the leader in that endeavor.

While Samira was smart, accomplished and grounded as a career woman and a dedicated mother, she was also a dreamer. A favorite refrain of hers was: "How constricting life would be, if it were not for the expansiveness of hope." She somehow maintained that perspective even through the war's dark years and its ravages on the psyche.

Other widows and single mothers were preoccupied with finding a man. Samira had no interest in what she called "such nonsense." Even though she had many suitors. She was a modern, independent, strong, confident woman, and luckily part of a loving extended family. Her main goal at this stage of her life was for her son to have a better future.

*   *   *

The future in Lebanon, with the Syrians occupying the country, was bleak. There were unknown yet inevitable problems yet to come. For Samira, having Dimitri sponsored by the Scotts was a dream come true, the chance of a lifetime. Yet, her joy was mixed with sadness and trepidation, knowing that she would not see her son during the years he would be growing into a man in a new world with a new culture on the other side of the globe.

Dimitri wanted to see the old stonemason Saleem one more time before leaving for America. The family headed up to the mountains for a long-weekend family reunion at Teta's ancestral village. When they arrived, Natoor's welcoming barks and sweet eyes filled Dimitri's heart with joy and love at seeing his trusty old friend. He broke out in affectionate giggles, hugging and petting the dog, who gave him a slobbering smile while wagging his tail. Dimitri had not been to the village in the past two summers during the war, and in the intervening years the black dog's muzzle had turned gray.

Dimitri felt comforted to be in a place that he loved so much and that had not changed, in dramatic contrast to the drastic alterations in the city over the past two years of civil war. Saleem and Najla came out to the balcony on hearing Natoor's joyful barks and added their own loving and welcoming vocalizations and dramatic gestures of affection.

"*Ahlan! Ahlan! Ahlan wa sahlan ya habayeb! Ahlan wa sahlan!!!*" Dimitri was immediately embraced by the couple. They had heard news over the past two years from Teta, who had often called her brother for solace, consolation and support while Dimitri was on the front lines.

The family sat down at the table for a reunion dinner that was a culinary feast of traditional foods with *kibi, tabouli, fatoosh, baba ghanouj, Humus, makdousi,* stuffed grape leaves and an assortment of pickles and savory bites.

After dinner, Saleem, Dimitri and Natoor headed out to secure the goats and chickens in the barn for the night.

"Is the fox still around?" asked Dimitri.

"The last time I saw him was in the autumn, he was frail but doing well. After the winter snow melt, I found him all curled up in his winter den that he created under the roots of the old baloot oak on the edge of the stone yard. He had passed away all curled up in his den under the thick winter snow. May we all be so lucky when the time comes. I covered him with cedar leaves and took some choice stones to seal his den, leaving him to rest in peace undisturbed."

The two walked silently back to the house, occasionally stopping to look up into the night sky starting to fill up with bright stars. As they approached the house, they saw Teta and Najla cross-stitching under the living room's bright yet warm yellow light.

"I hear you will be traveling to America soon," said Saleem.

"Yes, I'm both excited and sad about it. Being up here in the village, I feel like staying here. What do you think, *ya maalem* Saleem?"

"You are always welcome here. This is the land of your ancestors. But you are still young, and your future hasn't even started, even though you have probably lived what seems like lifetimes in the past two years."

Dimitri was comforted to know that someone understood.

"It's a great opportunity to see and learn from the new world," Saleem continued. "Be brave, make us proud to lift our heads when we hear your news. Know that you always have a stone cabin and goats in the mountains waiting for you."

Dimitri smiled. There is an old Lebanese saying: "Lucky and wealthy is the one who has a small patch of land and goats in Lebanon." There was something simple, basic, reassuring, comforting, true and timeless about that.

"I'm going to miss not being able to talk to you. There are so many questions and unknowns ahead, what should I do, who should I ask for advice and talk to in the new world?"

Saleem, in his familiarly calm but authoritative way, replied, "People complicate things. It's really very simple; just remember, Dimitri, wherever you go in this world and wherever your life takes you, seek to enlighten your mind and improve your character every day. If you do that, life will be good, and you will be fine"

Dimitri took Saleem's comforting words to heart. He felt his soul strengthened and protected by that simple, basic tenet, which he would make his guiding light into the future.

Dreams of a new world

In the late 19th and into the 20th century, America became a beacon of hope for the rest of the world. It represented a system and a vision for a more evolved and brighter future, with a spirit of optimism and hope. The principles it was founded on offered the promise of a place where freedom, liberty, separation of church and state, and the respect of the rule of law would allow for a sound life devoid of dictatorships, aristocracies, clans, sectarianism and a myriad of systemic ills that would keep a country stagnant and eroding.

The American University of Beirut amplified the Lebanese sense of the virtues and accomplishments that America offered the world in a very real, visible and tangible way, by graduating doctors, lawyers, engineers, scientists, economists, philosophers and writers who excelled worldwide in their fields of study.

There were also stories of many Lebanese Americans who had migrated to the new world and found success in a variety of fields. From renowned pioneering heart surgeon Michael DeBakey to America's first air force jet ace James Jabara, to consumer advocate Ralph Nader, to the artistry of master craftsman Sam Maloof, music pioneer Dick Dale, and actor Danny Thomas to name a few. So many Lebanese migrants had followed their dreams to the proverbial promised land and found success in diverse pursuits. The Lebanese spirit and initiative, combined with "the American way," created a driven, inspired, and contributing citizen.

America represented a sense of hope for the great and limitless possibilities that took one as far as one's imagination could travel and made the dream a reality by the extent of one's work ethic and dedication to that dream.

American movies further expanded the image that captivated the world's imagination. The rich and vivid Kodachrome colors in glossy magazines contributed to creating an indelibly appealing image of American life. For a young person coming of age, it was a very alluring picture of a future filled with boundless possibilities.

The day before leaving his homeland, Dimitri spent it saying goodbye to his friends. Heading back home from the neighborhood football field, he passed by all the stores in the neighborhood to say his farewells: first to Khawaja Joseph at the barbershop, with a proper haircut and send-off, followed by the bookstore to see Maalem Emile, who gave a book, titled *The Adventures of Huckleberry Finn.* Then to Hovik's photography shop and studio. From there he dropped by Mihio's toy and trinket store, his favorite as a child, a magical place filled with colorful glass and ceramic marbles, balloons, yo-yos, horns, kazoos, bird whistles, balls of all sizes and colors, toy cars, board games, cards, magic kits and so on. Then he dropped by the ice cream store for his favorite mango ice cream mixed with pine nuts. Then to Touma's for shawarma, a dish exported to Mexico in the late 19th century when some of Touma's ancestors migrated there, where it became known as *tacos al pastor.* Their shawarma spices and special recipe contributed to the flavorful culinary tradition of their host country.

Dimitri's heart was full, and he felt a responsibility to do well and properly represent all the people he loved.

* * *

Dimitri was ready two days before his departure. He had packed a coat, sweater, gloves and a wool cap, two pants, two sweatshirts, six t-shirts, underpants and socks, along with five meters of rope. Teta had taught him years ago, before his first Boy Scout camp, how to wash his clothes and dry them on a line. These things, plus a new toothbrush, nail clippers and a large block of olive oil soap from the village, all fit into the main compartment of his suitcase. In his left inside vest pocket, next to his heart, he kept a photograph of his family, with his passport, travel documents and an envelope of money. Teta sewed a strong and safe zipper onto the pocket.

The next day, before heading to the airport, Teta instructed everyone to keep their emotions in check. "No crying! We need to send him with confidence." This admonition worked all the way to the airport, until the loudspeaker announced the boarding of his flight, and the final hugs and kisses were exchanged. Then the floodgates burst open, the emotions and tears starting with Samira, followed by Teta herself and the cousins. The uncles stuck to the plan and put on a brave face with a smile while yelling out words of encouragement: "Make us proud, *ya habibi*."

Dimitri mustered a smile and responded, "Don't you worry, I will!" while turning away to join the herd of travelers heading to the far side of the airport to board a bus that would take them from the terminal to the plane parked out on the tarmac. Climbing the steps of the Middle East Airlines Boeing 707, with only four steps left before he reached the plane's door, Dimitri turned back to see his family one last time before heading to the new world and an unknown future.

Seeing them at a distance, clustered together, waving from the airport's terrace, Dimitri lifted his arm high and smiled with a full heart, capturing a photograph of them in his mind before turning and entering the plane.

From Beirut International Airport, the first leg of the journey would take him to London's Heathrow International Airport, where he transferred to a new Pan Am 747 jumbo jet that would take him to Seattle, Washington.

The first leg to London was quiet and somber as the weight of the moment sank in, before his thoughts gradually turned to sweet nostalgia, remembering Lebanon before the war. Summer memories of childhood and youth, diving and swimming off the rocky coast of Beirut. Riding bicycles, playing football, fishing, playing and joking around with his friends. The most profound memories were of those summers with the family in the mountains while working, building and learning from Saleem, the old stonemason.

When the captain announced the beginning of the descent into Heathrow, Dimitri came out of his nostalgic state of mind and transitioned into the present. He was alert, focused and on a mission to make it to Seattle without distractions. While following directions as he made the transfer to the Pan Am flight, he absorbed all the images and sounds of the journey with clarity and archived them in his memory, to be replayed and processed later.

*　　*　　*

Flying into the SeaTac airport, Dimitri peered out the window at the Seattle cityscape. From a distance, it looked similar to Beirut: a dense metropolis with clusters of buildings cascading down hills all the way to the shoreline of what looked like a large bay centered by a busy seaport, with ships coming and going.

One structure caught his eye, and he held it in wonder. It was some sort of futuristic-looking structure with three giant archer's bows planted in the ground and held together in the center. At the top of the bows was a flying saucer, or at least what Dimitri imagined flying saucers looked like, his only reference being the American sci-fi B-movies he'd seen at Abo Khalil's neighborhood movie theater in Beirut. His fellow traveler, a German sitting next to him, enthusiastically exclaimed, "Das ist Spaaace Noodle!" Dimitri politely nodded back even though he didn't understand what his fellow traveler was saying, he wanted to show respect, in that he shared in his enthusiasm and was equally impressed by whatever that thing was out there. Other passengers looking out the window verified the German's comment, clarifying: "That's the Space Needle." Dimitri made a mental note to investigate what that Space Needle was all about.

The enormous 747 made its descent, gliding with the magnificent grace of a giant albatross and touching down on the runway with a plume of smoke in its wake from its 18 tires hitting the runway. After a long roll, it headed back and taxied to the terminal. When the plane's door opened to the sky bridge, more than 500 passengers disembarked with Dimitri into a large building where they were greeted by signs and a map of the airport, with large electronic screens displaying departures and arrivals. Everything seemed on a larger scale than he had seen before. The plane, the airport, and even the people. In 1976, Seattle's SeaTac International Airport, with its subway train system, was one of the most modern and futuristic airports in the world.

Dimitri felt intrigued, awed and optimistic about this new world he was entering. It seemed so modern, orderly and predictable, a refreshing change from the disarray and chaos of a country at war. He noticed that a lot of thought and planning had been put into the airport's design to help move travelers and allow them to see, think, process and react intuitively. Aside from the pertinent travel information, he noted the plethora of alluring, oversized images everywhere, promoting all sorts of products in this new land of marketing and consumption.

While heading down a long corridor with travelers rushing by in both directions, Dimitri spotted a stout woman with a large, radiant aura standing in the midst of it all. She wore a short military haircut and an official-looking badge with the name Liz affixed to her uniform and a rainbow pin above it. Dimitri asked, in his thickly accented English, if he was headed in the right direction. "Excuse me, it's correct, no?" he said as he gestured down the long hallway with one hand and showed her his papers with the other: a letter from the American embassy with his sponsor's name and address, along with the requisite stamps and signatures. The official seemed amused; in a friendly, reassuring tone, she instructed him on which subway to take and what stop to get off.

"Thank you, thank you very much!" he responded, with his right hand on his heart and a slight bow of the head to her, before turning and continuing to the airport's subway shuttle, which took him to the luggage pickup area. After collecting his suitcase and going through customs, he came out into a large area where he spotted the Scotts waiting for him across a line.

A smiling Susan Scott, her eyes wide open with astonishment, stood with Professor Jim Scott, who waved vigorously while chuckling in disbelief. They couldn't believe how much Dimitri had changed from the 10-year-old boy they remembered. Equally astonished, Dimitri joyfully greeted them as they exchanged warm hugs. He was glad to have landed safely in the new world. It had been seven years since they last saw each other in Lebanon. The Scotts looked older, but at peace and happy.

James Scott was the youngest of three brothers born to a father who was an established dentist in his hometown and a mother who was a dynamic mover and shaker, if that expression can be applied to someone who was a pillar in her local church. But a mover and shaker she was, with a strong following. She was a bridge between the conservative women in her church and the progressive, educated and secular new generation of women emerging in her community. In a later era, she might have become the mayor of the town. But even without that sort of position or official title, she was instrumental in getting things done in her community, from changes in education to a wide array of civic action.

James's older brothers, Richard and Gilbert, had followed a prescribed path in life that was sound, albeit narrow and constricting at times. They did well in school, became successful engineers, married and raised families, while Jim, the youngest, was the black sheep of the family, the one who escaped their parent's demand to succeed in a conventional life. James went in a totally different direction, studying philosophy, theater and art. He became the official cartoonist of his State's University before receiving his PhD at Brown University in Providence, Rhode Island and returning home to take a professorship in philosophy at his alma mater.

Susan was the eldest of four born to a bright, ambitious farm boy from Virginia who rose rapidly in the ranks of the United States Navy after joining at an early age and fighting in the Pacific during the Second World War. Upon his return from the war, he married into an old aristocratic family. Susan's mother was a fair lady who ran a tight ship at home with the aid of domestic help.

When Susan was of college age, she rebelled against her parents by shedding her father's political and racial perspectives and her mother's high social expectations. As a student in her youth, she marched for civil rights and several causes that were on the right side of history and human evolution. Susan's quest to find her own meaning of life led her on an interesting path of privilege. She studied in Italy and Spain and took pastry-making classes in France before returning to study movement and drama at the University of California while attending an eclectic variety of seminars and workshops. After her world tour, she returned home to settle down in Seattle and enroll in college as an older student in a self-prescribed lifetime-of-learning program. It was during a rehearsal for a play that she met James Scott.

The two became active in the city's theater scene as well as a variety of social and political causes relating to justice, equality, human rights, gay rights, animal rights and protecting the environment. They were considered misfits in the conventional culture, with its focus on the economic boom, featuring seemingly limitless oil reserves, massive road and highway construction, and suburban sprawl traversed by the uniquely American gas-guzzling cars that were being churned out in record numbers in Detroit.

Like many misfits in history, the Scotts were simply ahead of their time. They were disillusioned with where the country was headed and wary of the many environmental, social and political problems that most people in power seemed to ignore.

Jim and Susan were looking for a change. Their openness to the world and their sense of service to humanity propelled them to move to Lebanon, where Professor Scott taught philosophy at the American University of Beirut during Lebanon's golden age. Dimitri's parents, at the time were students of Professor Scott, and helped introduce the Scott's to Lebanese culture, and to their family. Professor Scott became an influential teacher and mentor to Dimitri's parents, who both had a Western outlook, socially and politically. When Dimitri was born, Professor Scott served as Dimitri's godfather at the child's baptism.

The Scotts had no children of their own, but they possessed a generous and nurturing spirit evident in all their daily exchanges with people.

Driving from SeaTac Airport, Jim Scott took the long way home to give Dimitri a sightseeing tour filled with wonder at the new land he was to call home for the next five years. Heading towards downtown, they drove on one of the widest freeways in the United States. The thirteen-lane freeway was well engineered, pristine, clean and smooth, with large green signs that directed traffic to various branches of the city. Taking an exit into downtown Seattle, the Scotts drove onto the Alaskan Way Viaduct, a double-decker freeway that traveled through the high-rise buildings of the futuristic-looking metropolis facing Elliot

Bay and overlooking an impressively busy seaport that was open to the world for both commerce and culture.

The downtown streets were filled with pedestrians scurrying in every direction. The masses were well organized, with traffic and pedestrians following signs and lights that instructed them when to move and when not to. It was quite different from the organized chaos and freelance improvisations of Beirut's downtown that Dimitri had grown up with. Seattle's electric public buses whispered through the city's grid, picking up and dropping off passengers. Dimitri had never seen electric buses before, but he noted their similarity to the electric rail cars that had existed in downtown Beirut when he was a child.

"Are you hungry, Dimitri?" asked James.

"I'm okay, but yes, maybe a little," the shy and polite 17-year-old responded. Susan told him about her favorite restaurant in downtown Seattle, one that made falafel sandwiches "almost as good as the ones in Lebanon." The owners of the restaurant were a Palestinian and Israeli couple. Mahmood and Naomi were both open-minded, youthful optimists who met as law students at the University of Washington. After graduating and working in their field for several years, Naomi as a public defender and Mahmood in the business sector, they both decided law was not the career for them and decided to open a restaurant, while keeping their law licenses active. Both had been disowned by distant relatives when they announced they were getting married. But their immediate families, while proud of their Muslim and Jewish heritage, were also educated and enlightened. The parents not only approved but were happy for the young couple's genuine love for each other, and they celebrated the union with a sense of pride at having evolved.

Jim Scott drove his 1964 sage green Saab station wagon along a downtown street that crossed under an elevated railway on which an electric train travelled almost silently with a smooth whisper as it passed above. Dimitri had the feeling that he had landed in a very interesting, futuristic city.

Upon arriving at Mahmood and Naomi's restaurant, Professor Scott parked the car across the street and fed coins into a parking meter, adding to Dimitri's sense that this city was organized, orderly and predictable, something he especially valued after the chaos and destruction of the civil war.

As they entered the restaurant, the Scotts were greeted warmly by Naomi and Mahmood: "*Shalom,* professor*! Ahlan ya maalem*!" Mahmood waved them in, saying, "*Tfadaloo,* please have a seat," and directed them towards a table by the large window with a view of the monorail and the Space Needle. The Scotts introduced Dimitri to the restaurant couple, who were interested in hearing the latest news from the Middle East.

"Is the situation better now that the Syrian peacekeeping forces have entered Lebanon and the civil war is over?" asked Mahmood.

Dimitri had his doubts, but he kept them to himself, choosing instead to be deliberately optimistic as a matter of personal policy. He could only answer with "*Inshalah Kheir*" (God willing goodness). It was one of Dimitri's mantras, one he said often to others and privately to himself.

There was something about Mahmood that reminded Dimitri of his childhood friend Riad. The two were close friends during those years of blissful innocence, before tensions between the PLO and Lebanese Nationalists began rising in 1969. They played football together on the neighborhood dirt field with other kids from the adjoining neighborhoods, who were of mixed ethnicity, race and religion. Christian, Muslim and Jewish Lebanese kids played along with Armenians, Kurds, Palestinians and others that had sought refuge from the wars and persecution in their homelands and found an accepting, welcoming, progressive city in Beirut.

Riad's parents, who were both Palestinian, eventually saw the writing on the wall and left the neighborhood for a safer part of the city. Riad's mother, Leila, was a nurse who had been mentored by Teta at the Hotel Dieu de France Hospital and the refugee clinic of Tel al Zaatar, where Teta and Leila volunteered. Riad's father, Munir, was a teacher, writer and poet who stirred the ire of the Nationalists in the neighborhood with his political writings and poems. After a few incidents that brought on veiled and not-so-veiled threats, Riad's parents saw what was coming and moved to West Beirut.

The large neighborhood of Ras Beirut was a bastion of tolerance and peaceful coexistence. It began at the shoreline of the Corniche and spread upwards across the hills of the American University campus, then from Bliss Street up a gentle incline to Hamra and Commodore streets. At the peak of the neighborhood perched Beirut University College, overlooking the Pigeon Rocks to the west, with the lighthouse and the American University to the North. The area housed many secular professionals, among them professors, teachers, writers, journalists, poets, doctors, nurses, engineers, artists and businesspeople from around the world.

After the move, the childhood friends lost touch, as they grew into impressionable teenagers with political convictions during a volatile time in the country's history. They both willingly became indoctrinated into opposite sides of the brewing conflict, where each believed his own people's survival was at stake. Whether true or not, this hyper concern ultimately became a self-fulfilling prophecy. The civil war had put an end to a once innocent and beautiful friendship during the golden age of mid-20th century Lebanon.

For Dimitri, talking with Mahmood felt like setting back the clock … into the future. He started to think that Seattle could be a new chapter, a new blank canvas, with no layers of animosity or lines of separation.

Driving out of downtown Seattle, Jim Scott cruised along Westlake Avenue, its edge lined with docked ships and boats. After this scenic mile of the city's waterfront, they heard bells ringing incessantly and the traffic came to an abrupt standstill. "The bridge is up!" exclaimed Mrs. Scott, as the Fremont Bridge's two iron sections began to rise. The engineering marvels of their day stood in deference on both sides of the channel as a large, classic wooden schooner with traditionally rigged sails majestically made its way through the canal, with a myriad of smaller, well-crafted boats following it into Lake Union. While 20th century Seattle had a state-of-the-art road and freeway system, marine life and tradition still held a lofty position in the city's history and culture.

After the vessels made their way through the canal, the bridge returned to its horizontal position and traffic resumed in both directions. The Scotts and Dimitri headed up Fremont Avenue, past Lincoln High School, which Dimitri was to attend.

"This is where you will be coming tomorrow for placement tests. We already filled out the forms," Susan Scott explained. "Your new home is seven blocks down this street." After taking a right turn at Dick's Burgers, the sage green Saab traveled down Second Avenue and pulled into the driveway of a modest Craftsman-style house. It had a beautiful small garden where Susan found joy in spending hours cultivating a variety of flowers and bushes, she cleverly planted along a meandering walkway. Professor Scott maintained a collection of bonsai trees in an open shed he built on the side of the house. Dimitri's living quarters were in the basement but opened to the garden, with steps leading up to the kitchen of the main house.

Lincoln

The next day after breakfast, Dimitri reported to the neighborhood high school for placement testing. Lincoln High School was a large public school with nearly 2000 students, built at the turn of the century in the Victorian style. It was a solid, four-story brick building with a large gothic stone arch above its six front doors. At the northeast entrance was a large bronze bust of Abraham Lincoln and an inscription of one of his quotes: "Always bear in mind that your own resolution to succeed is more important than any other one thing." Dimitri held on to that quote as he approached the building. He knew he was entering a special place that would be instrumental in determining and shaping his future.

Stepping through the doors with curiosity, reverence and respect, he stood in the front hall, looking around and taking in the busy atmosphere of students scurrying up and down the staircases, heading to their classrooms. Within a few minutes, the halls were empty and silent. Looking around, he noticed the beautiful wrought-iron railing of the staircase, another confirmation that this was a special place built by master masons and ironworkers who took pride in their work. The school building felt sound and permanent.

Looking down the hall, Dimitri noticed doors with glass windows that opened to a large room full of light. Heading towards the light he was transported briefly to a childhood memory: walking up the nave of his church to take Communion. Reaching the end of the hall, he entered the room and stood looking at the rows of bookshelves and a large seating area, with a few small seating nooks in each corner. The large room was bright and filled with natural light from seven oversized, cathedral-like arched glass windows.

A woman approached Dimitri and asked gently if she could help. She stood straight, with a smiling face exuding calm confidence. The woman bore a striking resemblance to one of Dimitri's aunt's favorite singers, singer Billie Holiday. He noted her deep and soulful eyes, those of someone who has seen and experienced a lot.

Dimitri introduced himself and explained that he was here to take his placement tests. His old-fashioned formality and respect brought an amused expression to her face. "Your parents raised you well, young man," she said, catching Dimitri by surprise. It warmed his heart to think that his family was with him during this important foray into the new world.

The lady introduced herself as Roberta Byrd Barr and welcomed him to the Lincoln High School library. She explained that he should check in with the office down the hall to the right. After thanking her, Dimitri headed down the hall feeling fortified by his family's spirit within him.

Walking down the large empty hall, he entered the office and checked in at the desk, taking a seat next to other foreign students waiting to be tested. The door opened and Ms. Barr walked into the office, turning to the waiting students and wishing them good luck with a reassuring smile before entering her private office in the back. It turned out that the woman he'd taken for a librarian was the school's principal, though she had in fact been a librarian for years in the Seattle school district. In 1973, she became the district's first female and first black principal. Bright, inquisitive, and highly energetic, she was also a local media host.

Like many educators, she was a person driven by a higher, spiritual calling to inspire young people to learn, question and strive for a better life and a better world. She hosted a radio talk show for young children named "Let's Imagine" and a Seattle TV show that addressed social and political issues and possible solutions with her guests. She could be controversial, often interviewing people, such as Cesar Chavez, who were considered too radical for other shows.

Dimitri's test scores in algebra and geometry placed him at high school graduate level, eliminating the need to take math classes at Lincoln. The 17-year-old had studied both subjects in middle school before the civil war broke out. While happy to have aced his math placement test, it was surprising to him that a country that had put a man on the moon and a city that manufactured the best airplanes in the world, with a downtown that had a large flying saucer as its centerpiece, had a lower math standard than his school in Lebanon. But it seemed that the International Baccalaureate system that he took for granted in the old country was much more rigorous in certain key subjects. Math wasn't his favorite subject anyway, and he didn't miss being immersed in it. Although, as a young stonemason, he very much enjoyed and was a natural at geometry, or what he liked to call the visual mathematics of shapes and space.

In English, however, there was a wide gap for him to bridge. He knew only conversational English, which he'd learned watching American movies in Beirut. His vocabulary was enough to get by, but his accent got in the way at times, and he had to repeat things and use body language to fortify his speech, so he was placed with other foreign students in an ESL class, learners of English as a second language.

The classroom was in the Interlake Public School building, a block from Lincoln. The day before the first class, Dimitri scouted out his classroom. Walking up to the second floor, he noticed the craftsmanship of the wooden building, which was built by master carpenters in the mid 19th century. The beautiful grain of the stairs' hardwood treads was illuminated by a large, arched window that let in an abundance of natural light. The pattern and grain of each tread was a work of art created by nature and formed by the conditions and years of growth in a tree's history.

*   *   *

Dimitri found Room 202 and stood outside in the hallway, waiting for the class in session inside to end. At exactly 10 a.m. the door opened, and out came a girl who was obviously pregnant. Dimitri respectfully stepped back as she passed by. Then came another, followed by another, and on it went until the class was empty. Dimitri was both amused and confused at the unusual scene; apparently pregnant students were segregated from the rest of the school by putting them in a separate building a block away from the main campus. Many other classrooms and offices provided services to students who, in one way or another, did not fit into the mainstream of the student body. In that same building was an office for something called Planned Parenthood.

It all seemed foreign and a bit strange to Dimitri. But he was in the new world, with a new culture that he knew he needed to learn about and adjust to.

The next day, he entered Room 202 to be greeted by his ESL teacher, John Patrick Delahanty. There was something about Mr. Delahanty that reminded Dimitri of his French teacher back in Lebanon, Maurice Moreau. Monsieur Moreau had an old-school appreciation for the fundamentals, along with special gifts of intuition and sensitivity. He was thoughtful and patient with his students, yet strict in that he expected them to try their best. And they all did. Even the "delinquent," troubled kids were interested and engaged in Monsieur Moreau's class.

Mr. Delahanty had similar qualities of authenticity, empathy, and humor as well as high expectations. Although he looked quite different from Monsieur Moreau, who had been clean-shaven, immaculately groomed and possessed a ramrod-straight posture that remained from his days in the French army.

Mr. Delahanty was a gentleman poet and English teacher whose aesthetic included the same tweed jacket worn every day, with leather patches sewn over the worn-out elbows and a replacement button that looked different from the others but functioned just as well. He had wild, disheveled hair and an impressive mustache.

He typically wore a serious scowl that would turn into a sly, knowing smile that shone like a strobe light when a student got something right. In his class, stretches of focused learning were punctuated by moments of levity and hearty laughter that he instigated. The kids loved him and wanted to do well in his class.

That first day, Mr. Delahanty talked about his ancestors, who had migrated from Ireland and arrived in America by ship. He described the arduous journey and the difficulties they encountered, which made all the immigrant kids in his class feel that he understood their experience, anxiety and worry about being in a new country, especially one that spoke a different language than their native tongue. Mr. Delahanty did more than teach English, he gave them confidence that they could learn and succeed in the new world.

On his daily walks to and from school, Dimitri noticed that almost every block of the residential neighborhood had a workshop in one of the garages. On his own block lived Mr. Donaldson, an engineer by day and an inventor by night, with a few patents to his name. His son Keith had completely rebuilt a classic Austin Healey by age 16. It was becoming clear to Dimitri that there were a lot of unusual, smart, creative and innovative minds in Seattle.

Having been Saleem's stonemason apprentice, working with his hands and building since childhood, Dimitri was fascinated by the school's metal shop. Looking into the shop classroom, he marveled at the heavy-duty commercial lathe, bandsaw, drill press, miller, grinder, planer, shaper, and assortment of other machines and tools.

A man with a closely buzzed haircut welcomed him. Mr. Barta introduced himself as the teacher of the class and asked Dimitri if he had ever taken metal shop classes before. Dimitri told him about his bicycle in the old country and how he was inspired to turn it into an American Chopper after watching Bill Smith's biker movies, filmed in the California desert. Barta laughed and said, "I think you will find you are in the right place and that you will enjoy this class."

Dimitri's first assignment was to build a chisel from a rough piece of S7 tool steel heat-treated to RC60 hardness. After two years of prosecuting war's destruction, he found there was something therapeutic about working with steel and fire to produce something useful and permanent.

Dimitri's easygoing, friendly demeanor helped him make friends in the various classes he attended. At lunch break, he headed to the cafeteria, took a tray from a large stack and stood in a line that made its way into a lunch corral that guided the students through, like livestock heading to their troughs of feed. The different troughs were managed by ladies with hair buns covered by mesh caps. Ms. Alice, Ms. Stella and Ms. Judy were all older women. Ms. Alice and Stella were both grandmothers, yet they were called Ms. for some reason or another, as were all the female teachers, another curious thing that Dimitry made note of to ask the Scotts about at suppertime.

The lunch ladies, as they were known, presided over the food troughs, one for protein and grain, one for vegetables and one for Macintosh apples and milk. Dimitri, being from a culture that gave praise and thanks for the food and to those who prepared it, thanked each of them as he was served. He found it odd and rude that most other students just walked through taking food without acknowledging the lunch ladies. After making his way out of the line, he stood looking into the large lunch hall with his tray in both hands, hoping to spot someone he might recognize from class. When he saw someone familiar, he headed over to eat lunch with his new friend. Every day he sat at a different section of the cafeteria, depending on whom he recognized first.

One day his friend Tyrone, from history class, remarked, "Dimitri, I noticed you sometimes sit with the Chicanos, sometimes with the Blacks, sometimes with the whites and other times with the Asians." It was the first time Dimitri noticed that the cafeteria had indeed segregated itself in that way. As far as he was concerned, he was just sitting next to a friend. "Are you white, black or Chicano?" Tyrone asked.

"Me is We!" said Dimitri, without giving it much thought.

Tyrone gave him a confused look that slowly turned into a smile. "That's cool, brother," he replied and the two went back to eating lunch together.

At 17, Dimitri had jet black, thick and wavy hair, and a slight mustache. He had bronze skin from spending all day diving, swimming and fishing in the Mediterranean Sea the weeks before his arrival. He was hard to categorize according to the conventional racial divisions of the new culture.

As a newcomer he was lucky to have certain traits, some by nature and others by nurture, that shielded him from being picked on. While he had a joyful, peaceful and friendly personality, he also evinced a sharply stoic edge that others understood on a primal level: he was not one to have trouble with.

Growing up in Beirut and working at his uncle's shop, Dimitri had developed a deep reserve of street smarts. That, in combination with his physical training, made him confident of being able to navigate any situation or circumstance. He was able to keep his energy and thoughts unhindered by fear, anxiety or worry, instead filling that psychic space with a sense of wonder, optimism and hope. He looked forward to a bright future. Abraham Lincoln's quote at the school's entrance was a daily reinforcement: "Always bear in mind that your own resolution to succeed is more important than any other one thing."

Those first few months, over supper with the Scotts, he had the chance to have his curiosity satisfied. He was thankful to have thoughtful sponsors who had the time and interest to explain the culture he was becoming part of.

"How are you finding school here?" Susan Scott asked one evening. Dimitri, with palms turned up, tipped his head side to side, trying to offer an answer. "It's different here. There are different types that stay in groups with the ones that are like them."

"Oh, yes, those are called *cliques*. Which ones do you find interesting and want to make friends with?" asked Professor Scott.

"All of them. But I especially like the nerds. They are the purest of heart, true and clear. Greg is nice and has helped me with my schoolwork. He's also a brilliant chess player, the best in the school. We've had some good games during lunch, and he says that I should join the chess club."

"That's not a bad idea."

"I like playing chess. I haven't played chess since I was 13 years old, in 1972, when everyone in Beirut caught the chess bug and became obsessed with the Bobby Fischer versus Boris Spassky game, with each taking sides. That was at the height of the cold war. Chess replaced football at recess that year. But I can't join the club now. I need to keep working after school and send my mother money."

Jim and Susan looked at each other silently for an awkward moment then nodded. "That's understandable," Susan said, "but we just don't want you to miss out on a normal life for a boy your age. I'm sure your mother would want you to have fun and enjoy your life."

"Oh, it's okay. I enjoy working with my coworkers in the kitchen. They've struggled, lived and experienced life, and I feel like I have more in common with them than most of my schoolmates. Plus, I'm getting paid." Dimitri laughed.

"What about the jocks? Some of them can be bullies sometimes," Susan asked.

"Not the truly good athletes. They're confident and gracious. It's the second-tier ones that feel inadequate and pick on the weaker ones. I had to set a guy straight who was picking on Greg."

"Good lord! What did you do?" Jim responded; his eyebrows raised in alarm.

"Oh, nothing serious, I just pinched his radial nerve and had a talk with him. He's not going to bother Greg anymore."

The Scotts looked at each other in a moment of awkward silence.

"During lunch break in the cafeteria I beat all the jocks in arm wrestling," Dimitri continued. "Mike, Pete and Coach Hayes want me to play American football. It looks like fun, but I just don't have time to play games anymore."

The Scotts felt that Dimitri was more responsible and mature than many adults they knew. They respected his discipline, dedication and work ethic, qualities shared by many first-generation immigrants. But they were also realizing, sadly, how much he had been forced to grow up too quickly.

"What about the freaks?" Susan asked, hoping to lighten up the atmosphere. "I bet they're an interesting bunch."

Susan's life in the arts and theater gave her a special appreciation for unconventional creatives, a group she proudly considered herself to be part of.

"I like the freaks. They are the most interesting group. Although some are just indulged, privileged kids who seem kind of lost. I think they are looking for comfort by hanging out with other nonconformists, hoping they will be more empathetic and tolerant. But the interesting ones see the world more deeply and from different perspectives. I really like them. But they smoke a lot of funny-smelling cigarettes."

Jim and Susan looked at each other and giggled, prompting Dimitri to join in.

The Seattle public high school, a microcosm of the real world, was a good learning experience for Dimitri. Lincoln introduced him to many people from different races, creeds and socioeconomic backgrounds. During the school year his English significantly improved, thanks to the joy he took in reading. He excelled in woodshop and metal shop while doing well in other subjects.

The letter

Dimitri settled into his new community and looked forward to spending time during summer with his new American friends, swimming and diving off the floating jetty docks of Green Lake. He dreamed of finding a girlfriend with love in her eyes and flowers in her hair, of blue skies and warm lips kissed by sunshine, of holding hands and walking together in the lush green hills of Woodland Park on a beautiful summer day. He was feeling hopeful and optimistic.

The letter came in a blue airmail envelope with the words *par avion* stamped in French. In the upper right corner were two Lebanese stamps, one with a print of a cedar tree, the other of Roman ruins. Dimitri took a knife and gently opened the top of the envelope, making sure not to disturb its contents. He unfolded the thin paper and read:

Dear Son,
We all miss you very much. Knowing that you are doing well gives us hope and strength. Teta and I think and pray for you constantly. Thank you for your last letter. It made us all happy to hear that you are settled and finding Seattle to be a hospitable city and to your liking. We are all very proud of you, my dear.

Saleem made me promise to write this cryptic message to you. He said you'll understand: "The enlightenment of the mind and the improvement of character." He also told me to tell you that he and Najla miss you very much, as do all your uncles, aunts and cousins. Every time we are out in the neighborhood, one of your friends comes up to us to ask about you.

Politically things here continue from bad to worse. There has been a move to consolidate all the Nationalist militias under one new banner. They are calling it the Lebanese Forces. Your Uncle Victor thinks it's a good idea, but the way they are going about it is a disgrace and a tragedy. It's become fraught with assassinations and massacres of once-close allies who worked together and whose unity was key to defending our community.

As if that's not enough, the Syrian secret police are rounding up people on a list of Phalange suspects who have ambushed their tanks that were encroaching on our neighborhood. They came looking for your cousin Jabril, who is safe and in hiding up north in the village.

We are managing our lives while the economy takes another hit, and the Lebanese pound plummets in value to the dollar. Thanks to your Uncle Victor's store and his business acumen, we are managing. The important thing is that we have each other. The good news is that your cousins Elie and Fadi have graduated and are studying engineering at the university. Aunt Diana and Uncle Tony have a new baby girl they named Lina. She is a strong-spirited little thing. Life with all its difficulties continues to move forward.

Your safety, happiness and success in the new world gives us strength and is a bright hope for the future. May the angels always look over you and protect you, my dear son. Until the next letter, know that we think of you every day and send you all our love.

Your forever loving mother, Samira.

Tears welled in his eyes on reading his mother's letter, before he transitioned to a somber and stoic mood, which then gave way to a surge of energy and determination. It was time to grab the bull by the horns.

Dimitri had been washing dishes at an eatery in the University of Washington district after school. The work gave him a level of financial independence that made him happy to be able to send money back home, even if it was a modest amount. Every two weeks, he would use half the cash he had earned to buy a postal money order, which he mailed to his mother in Lebanon.

The next day at school, during metal shop class, Dimitri asked Mr. Barta if he knew of any machine shops that were hiring. He explained what was going on in the old country and that he needed to work full time to send money back home to his mother and grandmother. The teacher had taken an interest in Dimitri early on. He liked the kid's sensibilities, initiative and work ethic, which reminded him of a different era during his youth.

Looking nostalgically into some imaginary distance as he pondered the question, Mr. Barta nodded. "I had a dear old friend, Earl, God rest his soul, he was a machinist at Boeing for over thirty years. Earl was nearing retirement when I was just starting up at Boeing as a young man. He taught me a lot. Earl was a good man. His eldest son, Andy, has a machine shop in Ballard, and I think they might be looking for a welder." Mr. Barta wrote down the address and phone number, along with a simple hand-drawn map to the shop and the bus number, 46, that would take him there. "Tell Andy I sent you."

"Thank you, Mr. Barta. I have a bus to catch."

Dimitri's heart raced at the possibility that he could soon be working in a well-paying job and sending money home. He hopped on the 46 bus and sat by the window, looking out at the many industrial shops all along Lake Washington's ship canal. Reviewing Mr. Barta's map, he pulled the cable to ask for a stop, thanked the driver and stepped down onto the pavement, with Andy's Iron Works in view.

Entering the front door of the shop, he introduced himself confidently and asked to see Mr. Andy, which drew guffaws and bantering from the crew.

"Where is Mr. Andy?"

"Have you seen Mr. Andy?"

"Who is Mr. Andy?"

They kept saying "Mr. Andy" repeatedly. Dimitri wasn't sure what was so funny, but patiently stood and smiled, waiting for an answer.

A spectacled man in a blue jumpsuit, sporting half a dozen pens and a micro imperial/metric caliper in one chest pocket and a note pad in the other, emerged from the back of the shop and extended a hand to Dimitri.

"I'm Andy. Don't listen to these jokers."

The shop's crew was a tightknit group of machinists who had worked together for a long time. A couple were older than Andy and had been coworkers and good friends of his father Earl. The shop was impressively equipped yet seemed to have a sense of familiarity and ease among the machinists.

"Barta called and told me about you. He tells me you're a good welder and a hard worker."

"Yes! I always try my best, and I learn quickly."

Andy turned to his crew and admonished them with a smile. "See, that's what I'm talking about. I like this kid's attitude! Come, let's see you weld."

Dimitri suited up and was soon laying down a smooth, uniform, even and consistent bead of molten metal. After flipping his welding helmet up, he turned and looked at Andy who was smiling and nodding approvingly.

"Very good! The job pays five dollars an hour to start." That was twice the minimum wage but half what an experienced welder made. It was a great start, one that Dimitri enthusiastically accepted.

Andy's Ironworks machine shop

The summer after graduating from high school, Dimitri worked long hours, taking time off only to eat and sleep before returning to work early the next day. He was young, energetic and driven by love and a duty to help his family. While his young, tireless physical being was in Seattle, his heart remained in Lebanon.

Andy was a good boss, respected for both his knowledge and character. He approached each assignment with great care and focus, starting with meticulous planning and precise follow-through on each stage of the project. Dimitri knew he would learn a lot from him. Each machinist took pride in perfecting his part of the process. Along with a high standard set for each worker, there was a great camaraderie and morale in the shop

Andy worked often with an old friend and regular customer, David, building a variety of custom pieces for the many restorations and inventions David came up with.

In their teenage years, Andy and David had been on a team that won the All-American Hydroplane Crew of the Year award. Hydroplanes, also known as thunder boats, were a major part of Seattle's marine history and culture. The futuristic looking speed boats blended two of the city's top industries, aviation and boatbuilding. Every summer on Lake Washington hydroplane builders competed in a race that was part competition and part community extravaganza, complete with barbecues, baseball, beer, live music and kite flying. The aviation industry was the main source of engines for hydroplane speed boats. In the early days, it was World War II-era V12 engines, mostly Rolls-Royce Merlins and Griffons. Teams later started using Vietnam War-era turboshaft engines from helicopters like the CH-47 Chinook, creating a hydroplane that glided over the water with over 3000 horsepower.

Americans are crazy! an awestruck Dimitri thought to himself. In all fields Americans seemed to have a limitless imagination, with a strong spirit, belief, confidence and courage to make it happen. They were qualities he admired and identified with. Dimitri liked to point out that America's first air force jet ace was a Lebanese American by the name of James Jabara, a historical statement that came from both pride in his heritage and confidence in what was possible in the new world.

David early on had struggled with dyslexia, yet he'd landed on the honor roll throughout his academic life. His disability turned out to come with an interesting gift: he was able to see things in a unique way and from various angles simultaneously, making him a talented industrial designer. When Andy was faced with a difficult and unusual flow problem with aerodynamics or sequencing, he would often say, "This is a question for David." His friend was blessed with a first-rate mind, a creative outlook, physical stamina and a strong work ethic. David was also a self-proclaimed health nut who started his day at dawn, rowing a single scull on the predawn, mirror-like surface of Lake Washington before heading to work.

In David, Dimitri saw an admirable example of a self-actualized man living out his full potential, combined with an appealingly modest, old-fashioned politeness and decorum.

David's latest project was designing a rowing exercise machine that worked with human physiology. His first prototype, built at Andy's shop, offered fluid and continuous resistance throughout the complete range of motion and became a hit in the 1980s, when public interest in modern fitness was in its infancy. After several institutions placed orders for David's new rowing machine, he decided to roll out his other drawings and put all his designs into production by starting a fitness equipment manufacturing company.

He hired Andy to build a prototype fleet of heavy-duty commercial exercise machines, and Dimitri became part of the fabricating team dedicated to the new venture. After a year, the business had expanded considerably and had to move to a larger manufacturing space at an old shipbuilding dock and warehouse down the street from Andy's shop.

Dimitri, Andy, Joe, Anthony and John all invested their savings into buying shares in the new venture and rode on the first wave of America's 1980s fitness craze. What had once been a subculture, became mainstream with new gymnasiums and fitness centers opening in every city and town across America.

Dimitri, with great appreciation and thanks to the Scotts, moved out of his basement room and rented a small apartment in Ballard that was walking distance from Andy's machine shop. Life revolved around his work and his quest for the perfect weld each time he picked up the torch. The job paid well, and he took pride and joy in perfecting his skill.

There was no time to waste and no time to indulge in anything that took his focus off his path towards building his future while helping his mother and grandmother back home. His social life was almost nonexistent, generally limited to hanging out with his shop crew on Fridays after work for the fish fry and beer at the pool hall before heading to his apartment.

However, nature sometimes has a way of overriding a young man's most disciplined plans. Vicki, the waitress at the pool hall, was a looker. She and Dimitri became an item. Vicki found Dimitri pleasing to the eye and a far cry from her ex-boyfriend, the physically and mentally abusive Jake, who skipped town months earlier after a particularly heinous abusive episode. It took a while for Vicki to adjust to her new reality and make some changes in her life. She told her friends at the pool hall that she felt safe in Dimitri's strong yet gentle arms.

After an absence of months, Jake showed up at the pool hall one Friday night, drunk and amped up on something, and started to create a scene. Dimitri calmly walked up to Jake and looked through his eyes and into his soul. "It was the weirdest thing," Fred, the bartender and owner, recalled later "It's as if Dimitri had Jake hypnotized." Dimitri saw all that he needed to see and turned calmly toward Vicki who was standing next to Fred and whispered into her ear as he passed by: "Bring Jake out to the alley behind the kitchen. I will be waiting to have a talk with him."

With a nod and wink from Fred, Dimitri headed to the alley and waited, keeping the back door and an eye open. When he saw Vicki and Jake approaching, he moved away from the door. Jake stepped into the alley and was surprised to find Dimitri there, who motioned silently with his head for Vicki to leave. She quickly went back into the kitchen and locked the door behind her. Jake never showed up at the pool hall again.

Vicki had been sober for eight months, and Dimitri was starting to think of her as his beloved while entertaining plans to ask her hand in marriage in some old-fashioned way. Their relationship was passionate, affectionate, natural, and filled with all that matters and is desired by a young couple. But Dimitri couldn't shake off the nagging feeling that something basic was missing. Or that it was buried beneath several layers from her dysfunctional upbringing and adult relationships. He convinced himself he should be patient and let time and love cure all.

The couple were in the happy deep fog of love for eight months. Then one day, Vicki abruptly and without notice simply picked up with her girlfriend Crystal, aka "the snow queen," a lost poor rich girl with a trust fund that had fueled her addiction and that of her co-dependent friends. The two women skipped town together, leaving Dimitri hurt, confused and feeling foolish. He also felt a deep loss and sadness for Vicki, who, after a long period of sobriety, was now back racing towards oblivion.

His coworkers, all in stable marriages and relationships, behaved like uncles and older brothers, consoling him and assuring him he would find the right one someday. Not one to wallow in self-pity, Dimitri bounced back with a renewed commitment to building a sound future. His new mantra became: "Your future is created by what you do today." It helped him stay focused on the present instead of wallowing in the past and allowed every new day to start with hope.

The American

In the winter of 1981, after being in the United States for five years, Dimitri became an American citizen. Taking the oath of allegiance was a monumental and joyful event. He felt committed and validated by his adopted country. There was a sense of belonging to its future and of being part of a new generation of immigrants that infused the country with vitality and a positive spirit that made America truly great.

It also meant he could travel freely and go back to visit his family.

Mixed emotions came to the surface as Dimitri prepared to travel to Lebanon. He couldn't wait to see his family and his old friends. He also felt a bit sad to be leaving behind his friends in Seattle, even though it was just for a few weeks. After all, the city had been his home for five years, and his friends, in particular his coworkers, had become an extended family of sorts. When the day came and he boarded the plane, Dimitri was filled with excitement and anticipation, as well as pride at having made it in the new world. He couldn't wait to tell stories about his experiences in the United States.

In London, he transferred to a Middle East Airlines Boeing 707 that flew across Europe to the old country.

As the plane started its descent, the captain played a song on the sound system by Lebanon's iconic singer Fairuz, "Ya Tayr," a song that plays on the heartstrings of every Lebanese in the diaspora. The passengers' eyes welled up with tears as they peered from the windows at Lebanon's coastline. The plane flew above the Pigeon Rocks into Beirut's International Airport.

The moment the plane touched down, the passengers broke out in a loud cheer, "Yaeesh Lubnan!" and began clapping. It's a Lebanese thing that speaks to the special, heartfelt bond the people of this ancient land have to their homeland. Some openly and uncontrollably wept with joy. It was not only joy, but something much deeper.

As Dimitri descended the steps to the tarmac, the humid air of summer infused with the salty sea breeze told him he was home. He was in the natural environment he had grown up in. Seeing his family at a distance further expanded his heart. He rushed over to his mother, Samira, and the rest of the family and exchanged more heartfelt hugs and kisses in ten minutes than he had over the past five years.

The drive back home was filled with mixed emotions: the joy of being with his family and consternation at the reality he was seeing around him on the streets leading to his old neighborhood. Neglect was rampant. Buildings and roads were eroding, while the normally boisterous spirit of Beirut residents had dimmed, at least in public. Everyone was guarded in what they said. Tensions were high, with the Syrians still occupying the country and exerting control through their secret plain clothed police, who were not so plain or hard to pick out, with their trademark black leather jackets. Things still felt deeply unsettled, with various forces in flux. People sensed that the political deck was about to be reshuffled.

Even so, walking the streets of his old neighborhood, Dimitri's heart was filled with joy at seeing old friends and the people and shops of his old neighborhood. Everyone welcomed him with typical demonstrative Lebanese warmth and hospitality, happy to see their native son back. Everyone wanted to hear about America. They were all starved for stories that would take them away from the political realities of their daily lives and the difficult times they were experiencing under the thumb of an occupying army.

Some things hadn't changed since Dimitri left. Though everyone was a little older, they still had that Lebanese optimistic spirit of "Inshalah

Kheir."

Following the 1975-76 civil war of five years ago, Lebanon continued riding on a political roller-coaster of mayhem, betrayals, deceit and assassinations, with every group becoming more insular and extreme, while the country became more fragmented. Each faction put its own interests above the rest, and loyalty to their leader and warlord above the interest of the country. While the theater of democracy continued to play out in Parliament, the reality was that the country had regressed into modern-day tribalism.

It was only when visiting Saleem and Najla in the village that Dimitri truly felt he was in the Lebanon of his childhood. The mountains and their people retained the authenticity Dimitri had grown up with.

Spending time with Saleem and talking things over with him offered a true and trusted check of the experiences he had gained over the past five years.

After dinner, Dimitri and Saleem went for an evening walk to visit Saleem's old dog Natoor's grave. Along the way, they came to the cabin they had built together years ago, starting when Dimitri was 10 years old and first became Saleem's stonemason apprentice. The two stood there, reflecting on fond memories of working together in the years before the civil war. Dimitri pointed to the arch above the front door, with the keystone carving of *Dar Al Salaam*, house of peace. Saleem smiled with a look of admiration at the carved stone. "That sentiment is set-in stone by your hand years ago, and it will always be."

The two continued on the path leading to Natoor's burial site. The dog's finely carved tombstone stood in line with older tombstones Saleem had carved as a child, well over half a century ago. The old stones were weathered, but you could still clearly read the names of the various beloved animals, among them a favorite goat during Saleem's childhood, named Amalthea. Below her name was a carving thanking her for the milk she provided for the family.

Both stood silently, feeling reverence for the beloved creatures of the past. "This is life," Saleem said with a peaceful smile. "We are all in a queue that only moves forward. Some are ahead of others, and some are behind others, but ultimately, we all reach the same place." It was a simple, clear image, and acceptance of the temporal nature of life.

The new tombstone bore Natoor's name and an inscription: Love, loyalty, fidelity, camaraderie and courage. "That was Natoor!" Saleem said. "Humans could learn a thing or two from that dear old dog."

Walking back up the hill together towards the house, Saleem broke the silence with an upbeat question. "So, tell me, how did you find America?"

"I found the people to be nice and welcoming. You are free to do whatever you want if you follow the law. There is a sense of clarity and predictability. If you have a dream and the desire to learn, work hard, establish a good reputation and deliver, then you can make it there, even thrive. There are problems, but there are many good people like the Scotts who join in political action to bring awareness to important political, social and environmental issues. America is constantly evolving, which I think is the secret to its success. It's not stuck in the past."

Saleem nodded. "Evolution is the natural path forward. But remember, as you build upward to the sky of endless possibilities, make sure your foundation is solid underneath you. Without a sound foundation, the gains will be nothing more than an exercise in novelty, egotism and vanity that will ultimately fall. Anything meaningful and enduring starts from and continues to evolve from a sound foundation."

Nodding his head in agreement, Dimitri said "Thanks to you and Teta, my foundation is sound." Saleem smiled broadly. He had not sought that acknowledgement, but it made him happy and proud that his influence had made a difference in Dimitri's life. The sort of acknowledgement every parent, teacher or mentor finds meaningful and satisfying to hear.

*   *   *

The two walked together through the stone terraces where apple orchards curved in long rows around the mountain. Dimitri inspected and spoke to the trees the way he would with old friends he hadn't seen in a long time. He was happy to see the trees doing well and congratulated them on the new branches they had developed.

Walking around the curve in the mountain, Saleem pointed to the end of a stone terrace. "Remember that corner wall and stone steps? We built them the last summer you were here, before the war. They are still sound and standing strong, just like you."

The two smiled quietly at each other; a silent moment charged with emotion. It was the kind of approving, confidence-inspiring compliment a father would give his son. Saleem was the closest thing to a father Dimitri ever had, and the years of being his apprentice had taught him some fundamental life lessons. It was where the foundation of his character was built.

The old stonemason and his apprentice started to make their way back to the house, walking through the old stone yard, past the tool shed and the workbenches under the old baloot oak tree where Dimitri had first learned to work with stone.

He remembered those years like a nostalgic movie playing from his mind's memory bank. From his first lessons at age 10 until the final carving of the keystone with the words *Dar Al Salaam* and placing it at the top of the arch before removing the form and allowing the arch to hold itself indefinitely. It seemed like a very long time ago. So much had happened since then.

Through this visit he was learning that going back to where it all started has a way of confirming who you are, what you are, and why you are the person you have become.

Resting on a rock on a hill overlooking the valley, Saleem and Dimitri looked out into the distance past the Kadisha Valley at the setting sun dipping into the Mediterranean. As the fleeting orange and purple colors of dusk began to fade away, Saleem lifted his left arm and pointed to the west while his right hand remained planted firmly on the rock beneath him. Turning to Dimitri, he said, "You are now a citizen of the new world far out there. Don't forget where you came from." while he tapped the rock beneath him that emerged from the earth's crust surrounded by ancient cedars high up in the mountains of Lebanon.

"You have made us proud, *ya habibi*. Your life is ahead of you."

Saleem had lived a full life without feeling the need to leave the village of his birth, but he knew Dimitri had become a part of the brave new world out there and truly belonged to it.

As the two neared the old stone house, they could see Teta, Najla and Samira working on their cross-stitch. After all these years, this peaceful, meditative practice was still a nightly tradition for them to practice before turning in. Dimitri borrowed a book to read from the home library, while Saleem brewed chamomile tea for everyone before taking a seat at the dining room table and penning a few words with black ink on paper in his daily calligraphy journal.

*   *   *

The next morning, Dimitri accompanied Saleem to the village square shops to pick up a few items for Najla, while greeting and being greeted along the way by villagers and various shopkeepers. "*Sabah el kheir,*" morning of goodness, one would say, while the other responded with "*Sabah el noor,*" morning of light.

The two entered the village bakery, run by a stout woman with a radiant smile. Saleem proudly announced: "You remember Dimitri, my sister's grandson? He's here visiting from America."

"*Smalla! Smalla!* That's you, Dimitri? You're a young man now. That means I must be getting older than I thought."

"Not at all. You look just the same, Madame Randa."

Madame Randa laughed out loud. "Bravo! Bravo! Dimitri, you know what to say. You made my day."

Saleem and Dimitri laughed along with her. They picked up a half-dozen manouches to bring home for breakfast, but not before Madame Randa gave Dimitri a big hug and kissed his cheeks leaving marks of affection and white flour on him.

*   *   *

Despite all the changes in Beirut, the village was still the same. Everyone did their part and took care of the community, as they had for centuries. One sad difference was the rising number of portraits posted on a wall in the village square of young men who had died fighting in Beirut. Dimitri recognized several of them from his days as a Boy Scout in the mountains and a few from the days of standing alongside them in the streets of Beirut before he migrated to America. Some of the portraits from the 1975-76 war had begun to fade, having been exposed to years of rain, wind, snow and sun. Others looked recent and fresh; pictures of young men smiling joyfully and optimistically during what should have been the beginning of their lives.

The next day, Dimitri woke up to the much-missed sound of the rooster announcing the start of a new day. After breakfast, good-bye hugs and kisses were exchanged by all before Saleem handed Dimitri a linen bag with a drawstring. Inside were seeds of Lebanese cedar trees (*Cedrus libani*), from Saleem's collection. These seeds were part of an ongoing effort to collect, plant and reforest the mountains and valley with cedars. Every day on his walks, Saleem would plant a couple dozen cedar seeds. "Take these and plant them in the new world," he told Dimitri. "It's a blessing to whatever place they take root in."

*   *   *

Dimitri returned to Seattle with a renewed determination to forge his future with both feet planted in the United States, even though he knew his heart would always remain in the mountains of Lebanon. The blessing of his family gave him strength and furthered his conviction to make his life and future in America.

It felt good being back in Seattle with his adopted family at Andy's Iron Works Machine Shop. During his absence, a record number of orders had come in for gym equipment. The shop was backlogged with sales and orders for new commercial equipment, with sales on a rapidly rising trajectory. Work was plentiful and business was booming. New welders were hired, and Dimitri became a shop foreman.

Three years later, in 1984, the company was acquired by an international conglomerate, and everything changed. The fitness equipment company's "A" shares were traded on the London and Helsinki stock exchanges, and the close-knit machine shop and warehouse was shuttered in exchange for a new factory abroad that manufactured gym equipment on a large scale, with high-tech computer design and state-of-the-art manufacturing utilizing robotics.

Andy hung on for a couple of years, keeping his staff and taking on a shrinking number of small custom jobs before closing the shop and retiring. Members of the team who hadn't invested in the company had to find work in other shops. They were all skilled and experienced machinists, some with families they needed to support. But machine shops in the 1980s were typically not hiring, and those that remained open were laying off workers as manufacturing companies riding the tidal wave of the global free market shifted their operations abroad, where labor and raw materials were cheaper, and robots replaced skilled machinists and welders. It was the beginning of a difficult time for labor and unions in the United States that was destined to change the work culture, making it difficult for a tradesperson to own a house and raise a family.

Andy's kids were all grown; one was a public-school teacher, the other an engineer. Andy could finally fulfill a dream he shared with his wife to sail down to Argentina and visit her family. He and Sofia took to chasing summer year-round, up and down the Pacific Coast between Argentina and Seattle, in a large catamaran Andy had been building in his backyard for over two decades.

David, the maverick, took the lion's share of profits from the sale and poured himself into new projects. David always had many irons in the fire.

Dimitri was sad that an era had come to a close, yet he was looking forward to the next chapter in his life. He had always enjoyed David's aphorisms, especially the one that went: "Life is made of many chapters; don't get stuck on the same chapter all your life." And another: "If you are still the same man at 50 that you were at 25, then you have wasted half your life." David's sayings felt inspirational; they spoke of courage, hope, evolution, mental and emotional progress, always improving, and embracing what's ahead.

Dimitri cashed out his shares and sent half of the proceeds to his mother, who paid off her apartment and was able to take care of Teta's needs in her old age. With the other half he decided to seek his next chapter, starting with a road trip he had been dreaming of since arriving in America. The trip would take him south along the Pacific Coast before turning east into the deserts of California, then heading up north into the Rocky Mountains of Colorado.

Dimitri found a camper for his truck in the Seattle *Post-Intelligencer*'s Sunday classified ads. It had belonged to an old couple, George and Linda, who were avid bird watchers and had traveled on weekends throughout Washington State documenting its bird population. George had become medically homebound and had to put the truck camper up for sale while the two made do with watching birds through field binoculars from their porch.

George and Linda were rich with life experiences, generous of spirit, and enthusiastic about sharing their knowledge with Dimitri. George gave him a map of the Pacific Coast and pointed out the best places to go birding and camping. Sometimes in life, one briefly meets people in passing who remain a bright light in one's memory. George and Linda were such people for Dimitri. He hoped he would be so lucky as George and Linda had been, finding someone to love, appreciate life and grow old with.

In preparation for his road trip, Dimitri replaced the tires, hoses, belts, brakes and shocks, and changed the oil in both the engine and transmission. He placed a set of wrenches and a kit to fix flats under the passenger seat and mounted his bicycle on a rack he custom-built for his truck. After customizing the camper, he packed his water, food, favorite eight-track cassettes, clothes, a propane cooking stove, shovel, Winchester rifle and fishing rod.

During his last supper in Seattle, Dimitri was glad to have the opportunity to bid farewell to all his friends and mentors gathered under one roof at the pool hall. It gave him the chance to thank Jim and Susan for sponsoring him and taking the time and interest to guide him and teach him about the new culture he was becoming a part of. They were interested, thoughtful, and engaged sponsors who had his best interest at heart. Dimitri also thanked Mr. Delahanty, his English as a second language teacher, not only for teaching him the language, but also for making it his mission to encourage and instill in him the confidence that he will succeed in the new world. He thanked Mr. Barta for teaching him a trade that he can take with him anywhere in the world and make a decent living with. Then there was Andy, David, and the rest of the crew at the Iron Works Machine Shop, his extended family, who he shared his daily life with for the past seven years. It was a memorable evening that came full circle and brought an important transitional chapter in Dimitri's life to a close.

Pacific Coast

On the journey of life, as one window closes, another opens. Driving down south on Highway 101 to Oregon in a somber, reflective mood, Dimitri thought of all the good people he had met in Seattle. The culture was welcoming and an ideal introduction to his new homeland. People were well-meaning and helpful. He was given an opportunity, and he had made the best of it. Now it was time to find his own place in the sun.

As he drove down the coast, Dimitri took side trips inland to plant Lebanese cedar tree seeds that Saleem had given him, while saying a little prayer for the seeds to grow into healthy trees. Driving back along coastal Oregon makes for a lush, green, scenic journey, often hugging the foggy shoreline with ocean tides washing up on the rocks below, while at a distance a view of small rocky islands called sea stacks, emerging from the ocean and whittled by the erosion of wind and water over Millenia. The rocky islands stand like sentinels of time watching over the Pacific Ocean's ebbs and flows.

Pulling into a campground, Dimitri set up his camper for the evening before taking a walk on a stretch of beach dotted with driftwood: juniper, alder, willow, maple, and even the native cedar.

Contemplating the beauty of driftwood always comes with an element of sadness, with the recognition that it all began long ago with a determined little seed that burst through the earth and looked up to the sun as it grew into a sapling, its arms reaching for the sky. Through many seasons of trial, experience and adaptation, it developed into a robust, mature tree that had witnessed decades and even centuries while sheltering thousands of birds and other wildlife. Ultimately, like all living things, it grew old and reached the end of its life, falling into the river and going down stream on its final journey towards the vast ocean floating and being carried with the currents before finally arriving to rest on the shore.

After a long walk along the shoreline with the sound of the waves clearing the mind and nourishing the soul, Dimitri returned to his camper and lay down his head to sleep.

The next day, driving across the arch of Rainbow Bridge also known as the Bixby Bridge into Big Sur, felt like passing through a gateway; it was a place that seemed to span the gap between the humancentric life of cities and a timeless place unaffected by human ambitions. Standing on the rocky shore of Big Sur, surveying a panorama of limitless beauty, was a transformative experience. Dimitri stood in awe of its unspoiled natural beauty and the waves that had been unfolding on this shoreline for millennia. The ocean and the mountains remain the same, no matter the frenzy of human civilization.

Dimitri continued driving down the coast of California, with the ocean on one side and green, rolling hills on the other, dotted with gnarled old oak trees and young saplings bristling with potential, and sometimes fields full of flowering asparagus. All along the coast, the wind carried the scent of fine sea mist, while pelicans flew in single file, skimming the contours of the ocean's waves. Despite their odd appearance on land, they were remarkable flyers in the air, cutting through the mist while gliding gracefully across the cresting waves without moving a wing.

Reaching Los Angeles just before sunset, Dimitri was struck by how similar the geography and quality of light seemed to Beirut. After parking his camper by the beach, he made his way up to the Malibu cliffs looking out to the Pacific Ocean and took in the vast and expansive view, with the deep orange sun setting into the distant horizon. Down below, gray whales and their newborn calves could be seen gliding just under the water's surface. Occasionally, they would resurface to spout out a geyser, then fill their lungs with fresh air before diving back into the depths.

As night set in, Dimitri opened his camper's windows and lay down for the night, breathing in the fresh ocean breeze, while listening to the sound of the gentle, rhythmic and, hypnotic serenade of waves moving across the shore. As he drifted to sleep, he dreamt of the Pigeon Rocks of Beirut and his childhood friends fishing and diving into the sea, a nostalgic vision that would remain in his mind's eye forever.

At dawn, Dimitri's first stop was to the Los Angeles wholesale market. His friend Dennis from the Seattle fish market had told him it was worth a visit, as was Venice Beach. After parking his truck, he soon came across a food truck with a line of people queuing up, drawn by the aroma of Armenian spicy sujuk sausage, pastrami and eggs, which soon had him in line as well. The food van's proprietor, Petros, was an Armenian who grew up in Lebanon and immigrated to Los Angeles during the civil war. The two caught up on the latest news of the old country. Dimitri thanked him for the best breakfast sandwich he'd had in years and headed into the market, whose sounds and smells reminded him of Beirut's old souks during Lebanon's golden age. It was good to feel part of the mix of an awakening city again, and to feel he was contributing to its vibrant pulse at the start of a new day. The wholesale market is where goods and raw materials make their first appearance. Everything that follows is retail and consumption.

Making his way through the growing crowds of buyers for restaurants and neighborhood retail shops, Dimitri picked up a sack of almonds as well as dates, avocados and grapes, to add to his box of sardine cans from Seattle and the dozen fried and crispy pita bread loaves in a bag that Mahmood and Naomi had prepared and given him at the farewell party in Seattle. That, along with a twenty-gallon tank of water, completed his preparations for the next leg of the trip into the California desert.

From the foothills of the San Gabriel Mountains, overlooking the Pacific Ocean shimmering in the distance, one can still imagine the beauty of years gone by, before Los Angeles became overbuilt and scarred with grids, roads, avenues, freeways and sprawl filled with busy human activity. In the late 19th and early 20th century, Los Angeles was the heart of an agricultural area, with expanses of vineyard, citrus and avocado groves that stretched as far as the eye could see. The groves ultimately gave way to a modern metropolis.

Cruising through the city, Dimitri drove east into a residential neighborhood with homes that had iron bars on their doors and windows. They looked like self-imposed prisons. The streets were empty and still … too still. The eerie atmosphere told him instinctively that something was wrong. It felt like a prelude to something about to happen, or the post-traumatic state of stillness after something bad had taken place. Residents peered from behind the drawn shades of their homes while Dimitri drove through at a calm and steady pace, his hand on the stick shift and his left foot right over the clutch, ready for a possible sudden needed boost in torque.

Dimitri scanned ahead and behind with reptilian eyes as he drove down the street with all the smoothness of a crocodile making its way down the river, regulating his raised adrenaline and heightened awareness through the discipline honed during his time on the Green Line.

After rolling through the neighborhood without incident, he reached a busy intersection teeming with the normal flow of city life and the relative safety of numbers. He stopped to top off the gas tank, then walked into the gas station's convenience store and asked the old man behind the counter if he knew of anything unusual that happened in the neighborhood a few blocks back.

"Nothing unusual," the old man said abruptly. Then with a look of disapproval and pity, he shook his head. "You know, it's a shame, these young men today. They're energetic, strong, bright, and at the start of their lives, messing with that poison out there. It's killing them. Even worse, it's killing their minds and their souls while they are still alive. There are so many walking dead among us, so many walking dead."

Dimitri shook his head sympathetically while listening to the old man's rant. As he was to learn, the neighborhood marked the border between two rival gangs competing for their share of the profits from the crack epidemic of the 1980s. A drive-by shooting had taken place a couple of hours ago in a dispute over territory. Ambulances had just picked up the bodies and delivered the injured to a hospital and the dead to the morgue. After things were cleaned up and a police report completed, the neighborhood was left to return to business as usual until the next episode.

Dimitri noticed many contradictory and contrasting realities in Los Angeles. Just a few miles to the west along the coast was a whole other world; at the Santa Monica marina, multimillion-dollar yachts docked, and their occupants dined at three-star Michelin restaurants not far from the homeless population and surreal circus atmosphere of Venice Beach with its open-air stage of colorful and talented street performers, some with questionable mental faculties. Dimitri watched in disbelief, fascination, admiration and a cringe as a juggler fired up three chain saws and kept them on continuous auto-run while tossing them high in the air above his head, twirling and juggling them without missing a beat... or a limb.

Farther down, a fire eater swallowed a flaming sword and exhaled balls of fire while roller skaters danced and weaved to disco music; the self-styled sultan of skates, wearing a large turban and flowing white robe, skated and glided smoothly through the crowd while strumming a guitar.

The sultan of skates glided through the audience while watching a performance of acrobatics, calisthenics and isometrics by a talented and athletic acrobatic family of performers who formed a human column, standing on each other's shoulders, with the father at the base carrying the weight of four of his children on his shoulders. The fifth child, the youngest and lightest, climbed up his siblings and performed handstands and acrobatics at the very top of the human column.

Not to be outdone, the bodybuilders at the Muscle Beach's workout pit pumped iron, with the rusty metal plates clinking, clanking and ringing like the bells of a physical culture temple. The bodybuilders flexed their shiny muscles for the crowd. Some, slathered in baby oil, glistened in the summer sun, looking like puffed-up glazed doughnuts, while other, more seasoned iron athletes looked like classic Greek statues of Hercules carved in stone.

Next to the open workout pit stood a strong man known as the Magnificent Sicilian. Franco wrapped iron rebar around his forearms, creating iron coiled springs that he handed out to the audience. For a grand finale, he would tear the mammoth yellow pages telephone book with his bare hands and burst a rubber hot water bottle by forcing air into it with his mighty lungs.

Not far from this statuesque scene and feats-of-strength display was a talented street musician who rolled his upright piano out onto the strip, set up a donation jar, and proceeded to entertain the crowd with ragtime tunes, opening with the popular piece "The Entertainer."

Dimitri found Venice Beach's audiences as entertaining as the performers. There was the overfed and oversized Texan with a ten-gallon hat, whose wife was plastered with a thick, multilayered mask of makeup and garish shiny jewelry glistening in the summer sun. Her rhinestone bejeweled vest featured a portrait of Jesus wrapped in an American flag. The massive couple walked together, taking in the various shows, with a tiny Chihuahua enjoying a front-row seat in her purse. Amused, Dimitri watched them walk away and couldn't help but notice the woman had extravagant rhinestone crosses sewn into her jeans' back pockets, which caught the sunlight and flashed every time her massive behind shimmied.

Dimitri giggled internally while thinking of what Teta's reaction would be to this absurd narcissistic scene of religious affiliation and display. Teta wore her modest cross under her shirt. The only display of her faith was through her generous spirit and her daily good works, helping others.

While making his way through a sea of tourists, Dimitri noticed two beach nymphs parading around in not much more than string for a bathing suit and cutoff jeans designed to reveal more than conceal. The nymphs strutted like alley cats, drawing the watchful eyes of the crowd, including gangsters with teardrop tattoos adorning their faces. The tattoos started close to the edge of their eyes and extended down onto their cheeks. Some had a couple of tattooed teardrops; others had many, depending on the extent of their experience. The teardrop tattoos signified a lengthy prison sentence. A full ink teardrop signaled a committed murder, while an outline of a teardrop represented an attempted murder. Each neck bore the letters ELA, shorthand for East Los Angeles. The gangsters strolled along the neutral territory of the Venice Beach strip with stout, muscular thick-necked dogs wearing spiked collars.

Some spectators had interesting tattoos that were not so sinister, but rather masterful works of art. Many tattoos were just an overstatement of one sort or another that spoke loudly of a desperate need for attention. There were many lost souls and fallen angels roaming the streets of the City of Angels.

With his truck and spare gas tank refueled and his two twenty-gallon water tanks filled, Dimitri headed onto a road lined with eucalyptus trees whose scent mixed with the sweet smell of fresh baked tortillas. Heading towards the desert, Dimitri arrived in the quaint small city of Glendora, nestled in the foothills of the San Gabriel Mountains. Cruising along slowly, he took in the character of the old town until he came to a point where a dozen or so cars had come to a full stop behind a gate with flashing red lights and the sound of warning bells. From a distance, a tremor began to build, followed by the rumbling sound of a stampede approaching, and finally a solid wall of steel containers appeared, rolling by on thick iron wheels. Each railcar carried two large steel shipping containers from the Port of Los Angeles. Powered by six massive diesel locomotives, it was the longest train Dimitri had ever seen. The main route through town came to a temporary standstill while products from China made their way inland.

The mesmerizing continuous passage of double-stacked shipping containers appeared endless and went on for what seemed like an eternity before the train's hypnotizing sound faded into the distance and the steel gates were lifted back to vertical position with the red lights turned off.

Until recently, Dimitri had often marveled at the large commercial ships arriving at ports like those of Seattle and Los Angeles that carry thousands of containers each, delivering all sorts of goods from around the world. Historically, seaports have enriched the cultures of civilizations and helped create empires. There was something exciting about witnessing and being part of the 20th century empire that was America.

However, Dimitri was beginning to question things. He had noticed a shift in the culture during the 1980s, where there was seemingly an insatiable appetite for the latest "stuff," propelled by a multibillion-dollar marketing and advertising industry that spent all its energy enticing, convincing and manipulating consumers to buy things they didn't even know they needed, but now couldn't be without. He noticed that, for the most part the perceived need was more of an obsessive want than an actual need. This manic obsession with the latest products of convenience, image and style had made over-consumption one of the main pillars of the world's largest economy.

Dimitri thought of the old stonemason, Saleem, and what he had stressed about the importance of a sound foundation. No matter how extravagant and great a thing is, if it's not built on a sound foundation it is an exercise in greed, egotism and grandiose narcissism that will ultimately give way under its own meaningless weight.

While consumption rose, the quality of manufacturing had dropped.

Most products were now manufactured abroad: cheaply, quickly and in record quantities. They came with a built-in short life span, thanks to cheaper materials inferior workmanship. It had become cheaper to buy a replacement than to fix things at the rapidly vanishing repair shops. Instead of building something of high quality that would last, the new manufacturing model was focused on building products as cheaply as possible, with the aim of making them affordable to more consumers and, of course, increasing corporate profits.

The advertising and marketing wing of big business peddled a new and improved version of the same thing every year that made consumers hop on the hamster wheel of constant upgrading.

Landfills grew larger, as did the barges filled with junk and waste that were dumped into the ocean. The economy and rampant consumerism continued a steady climb, to the delight of big business, banks and the money changers of the stock market. So-called progress was in full swing. Convenience and ease in everything, from how people fed themselves to how they got around, created a pandemic of obesity physically and mentally. TV had become the new altar of worship in every American home, while the advertising industry preached to the masses about the ideal way to live.

Dimitri was questioning many ideas he had bought into while trying to fit into the modern world. He thought of Teta's brother, who had lived a healthy, happy, peaceful and fulfilling life of self-sufficiency in the mountain village of the old country and wondered if this kind of life could even be found in the world of progress.

As he was discovering, road trips are great for allowing the mind to wander and consider ideas that the routine of a busy "normal" life neglects, puts on hold or even deliberately and tragically severs at the altar of conformity to a conventional life. Too many people were too busy getting in debt, paying the mortgage, raising a family, and trying to get ahead while saving to take a vacation from it all.

Dimitri was looking for something different, something he hoped would be permanent and sound.. He wasn't sure exactly what that looked like, but he knew that he wanted a life that he didn't have to take a vacation from.

On a lone desert highway

Dimitri got onto Interstate 10, heading east into the California desert. It wasn't long before the traffic and busyness of city life was in the rearview mirror, becoming more distant by the minute. A vast world of peace and quiet was opening to him in the Mohave Desert. Approaching Joshua Tree Park was a magical experience, with the setting sun behind him casting its ancient boulders and barren formations in a deep orange glow. It was like entering a portal through time and connecting the spirit with a timeless reality beyond the dizzying, humancentric pace of a conventional modern life.

Humans have occupied the area of Joshua Tree for thousands of years, starting with the Pinto Culture, followed by the Native American Serrano, Chemehuevi and the Cahuila. In the 1800s, cattlemen drove their cows into the area and built water impoundments, while miners dug tunnels through the earth looking for gold. Homesteaders began filing claims in the 1900s and began building cabins, digging wells and planting crops. For better or worse, everyone who lived in the area left an imprint on it, while the Joshua trees and rock formations stood as sentinels, witnessing it all.

From ancient times, when cultures lived harmoniously with nature, to the advanced cleverness and destructiveness of modern humanity's ambitions ... through it all, the area has remained a spiritual oasis.

The Joshua tree, which grows only here in the Mohave, used to be called the *sovarampi* by the Pinto. The Cahuilla people called it *humichawa*, and the Shoshone called it *umpu*. For thousands of years, waves of new tribal groups embraced the tree as a spiritual reference and valued resource. In the 19th century, Mormon immigrants on their arduous migration west came upon the trees and named them after the biblical figure Joshua, seeing in them limbs outreached in supplication, guiding the travelers westward.

Along with the trees, unusual rock formations cover the landscape, giving it an other-worldly feel. Scientists have traced the birth of these formations back to over 200 million years ago, when volcanic activity resulted from the North American Plate colliding with the Farallon Plate under the Pacific Ocean. The friction from subduction caused the surrounding underground rocks to melt and form magma plutons. Over the years, the topsoil eroded, letting the granite rocks reappear at the surface and eventually settle into piles on top of each other as the softer earth crust continued to erode over time, creating the extraordinary rock formations seen today.

*   *   *

Dimitri spent a week wandering through the area. The experience expanded his vision of the Earth and gave more meaning to his time on it. It made him reflect on the limitations, pettiness and folly of the humancentric world of progress, competition, greed and war. The desert has a way of stripping away all human illusions and leaving one's soul bare and in total communion with the endless and timeless universe that is God. It became understandable why spiritual seekers throughout the ages and many prophets among them Abraham, Moses, Elijah, John the Baptist, Jesus and Mohamad, all spent quite a bit of time in the desert in communion with God.

As the sun began to set, continuing on the desert interstate over miles of open, parched wasteland, he gradually began to see a dim flicker in the distance. As Dimitri got closer, a desolate desert town came into view, with a lone gas station whose fluorescent lights transmitted a cold, artificial, flickering glow that was in odd contrast to the beautiful, peaceful, and warm colors of the serene desert sunset starting to form in the vast, open big sky.

Dimitri pulled into the station to refill his gas tank. While heading in to pay the cashier, he noticed from a distance what looked like a sack of russet potatoes. As he approached and got closer, he realized it was a stout muscular dog curled up by the cinder block shack. Gently and with friendly intentions, he squatted down next to the dog. It opened its eyes to look at Dimitri while wagging the tip of its tail. The dog seemed to have been through a difficult time, bearing not only physical scars but also a look of resignation. The two silently communicated together as Dimitri stroked the dog's flank gently, petting his head, and softly scratched behind his ear. The dog leaned his head into Dimitri's hand, wanting him to tickle his ear even more. The dog's acceptance of his affection seemed to suggest he was once someone's pet before being abandoned. Dimitri found it hard to imagine someone neglecting such a sweet dog. Inspecting the dog more closely, Dimitri noticed a shallow flesh wound, from what seemed like buckshot or possibly barbed wire.

"You stay here. I'll be right back," he told the dog as he rose and headed into the shop to pay for the gas.

"Good evening, sir, is that your dog outside?" he asked.

An old man with bronzed skin the texture of weathered leather and long, snowy white hair in a tight braid turned to look at him. His sunken eyes deep in his skull, and wrinkled face spoke of the volumes of life experiences and the many expressions that had left their mark on him. The old man replied in a low, deep voice: "So many wild dogs out there. Most don't make it past the coyote packs. The ones that do have to deal with drunk fools that shoot at them."

The two shook their heads in mutual disapproval and sympathy.

"Do you mind if I take the dog with me? I'll take good care of him."

The old man looked Dimitri in the eye. The two had a moment of quiet, intuitive and mutual recognition, as kindred spirits across cultures and generations do.

"You'll need to buy some dog food. I've been feeding him the past few days."

Dimitri bought a bag of kibble and a few cans of Spam. He inspected the dog for fleas and ticks. The desert was too dry for ticks. Using the water hose on the side of the building, he lathered up the dog using a bar of pine tar and cedar oil soap. The dog seemed a little nervous but trusting and happy with all the attention and affection he was getting.

"Okay, Spud, you're all done." The name *Spud* somehow stuck, and the dog confirmed it by wagging his tail every time Dimitri said the name. After drying Spud, Dimitri applied a mixture of turmeric and witch hazel to his wounds and fed him a dinner of kibble and Spam, with a bowl of water placed next to his food. Dimitri fashioned a cozy dog bed out of a sleeping bag on the passenger seat, and Spud readily jumped into the truck and curled up in his new bed, letting out a deep grunt and a sigh of relief and contentment. Spud intuitively knew his ordeal was over and that a new chapter had begun with a human he could trust.

The two made their way along the long desert highway, with no trace of humans for as far as the eye could see. Occasional gusts of wind would blow tumbleweeds across the sunbaked pavement.

Dimitri and Spud pulled over to take a stroll, before sitting down on a rock next to each other, taking in the serenity of the quietly beautiful scenery. An occasional whisper of a breeze would sweep over the desert's surface, carrying with it the dust of time and fine particles of the many lives lived long ago.

He sat pondering the absurdity of human ambition, competition, exploitation, power, greed and wars that have plagued civilizations, and were waged with uniquely human brutality by civilizations believing in their own righteousness as they conquered, slaughtered and subjugated under the banner of progress and enlightenment.

Dimitri was realizing that the accomplishments he had admired in empires of the past and the current American empire, with its spirit of limitless possibilities and ambitions, had a dark side. This was not a uniquely American trait, he knew, but rather a dark human trait that transcended time and place.

But here, the scale was on a different level. Like everything else in America, it was massive and extreme. From the genocidal treatment of the Native Americans to the abomination of slavery, to the scouring, drilling and destruction of the earth, and the so called "advancements" that lead to the creation of nuclear weapons that could end life on earth as we know it, America was in first place, number one, numero uno.

But it was also leading the world with inventions that saved lives, that expanded intellect and universal understanding. It championed human rights, tolerance, fairness and the creation of a roadmap to a better future for mankind … on paper. The actual implementation proved to be challenging and incremental, with mixed results and a constant need for awareness and struggle to live up to the ideal.

America had many contradictions, yet it continued to move forward, correcting itself along the way and, in doing so, keeping hope alive. Teta had always said, "How constricting life would be without the expansiveness of hope." America had expansiveness of hope built into its Constitution and embodied in a grand gift from France in the form of the Statue of Liberty.

*   *   *

After a long drive through the desolate desertscape, Dimitri and Spud finally arrived in Phoenix, a welcome sight to the desert traveler, a place to replenish, refuel and refresh. But Phoenix struck Dimitri as odd, built on a grid of unimaginative squares and rectangles, with endless rows of houses and lush, green golf courses irrigated with millions of gallons of water whose main source was the Colorado River. Phoenix seemed a modern, artificially transplanted city surrounded by the beautiful Sonoran Desert.

The first stop was to a veterinary hospital, where Spud's wounds were attended to, along with the recommended vaccinations. "There you go, buddy, you're all official now," Dimitri told Spud, who was wagging his tail, happy to be out of the vet's office with his human companion.

The Rocky Mountains

The two drove north heading to the Rocky Mountains. Dimitri was looking forward to seeing an old friend: Kevin, a photojournalist who had been stationed in Beirut during the 1975-76 war. On Christmas Eve in 1976, Kevin had taken a photograph of Dimitri holding the line at a sandbagged street fortification defending the sea port. During lulls in the fighting, Kevin and Dimitri would talk about photography. Kevin had shared his professional experience and tips with Dimitri, and the two became friends, exchanging addresses before Kevin was called to cover a brewing conflict in Mozambique. The two remained in touch and had written to each other every Christmas over the years.

Kevin's wife, Jenn, worked with the United Nations UNICEF relief agency, saving children in some of the world's toughest conflict zones. They both were unusual free spirits, saintly beings in Dimitri's view, with a deep love for humanity that spanned the globe. They had their home together in the mountain town of Nederland, Colorado.

Dimitri drove up the winding Boulder Canyon Road alongside Boulder Creek, where clear, sparkling waters coursed through the boulders in a murmuring melody. The beautiful view and peaceful sounds of the creek created a new state of mind that replaced the tension of rush-hour city traffic.

After ascending 3000 feet through Boulder Canyon, Dimitri and Spud arrived at the Barker Reservoir, a large body of water on whose banks nestled the small mountain town of Nederland, surrounded by the majestic mountains of the Continental Divide.

Nederland had the rustic charm of an old town that had gone through several reincarnations. There were no traffic lights or stop signs. People seemed at ease walking with their good natured dogs by their side.

"What do you think, Spud? Looks like a nice place for both of us."

When Dimitri arrived at Kevin and Jenn's home, he was warmly greeted, as was Spud by their dog Makenze.

The old friends stayed up late after dinner catching up on the eight years that had passed since Kevin was on assignment in Lebanon.

Dimitri explained how riding the American fitness craze and his long hours and hard work building commercial gym equipment got him to this point of realizing the American dream. "I am now on a road trip to find a peaceful place away from the city to settle down."

"I think you'll like it here," Kevin said. "It's peaceful and quiet, and the people have a live-and-let-live attitude." He also said Dimitri would find a lot of interesting and colorful characters in this mountain town and neighboring Sugarloaf, overlooking the city of Boulder.

*　　*　　*

The next day, Dimitri and Spud headed down the mountain into downtown Nederland, a one-block street anchored by the Pioneer Inn at one end and the Barker Reservoir on the other. The Pioneer Inn was an old-time, rough-hewn wood bar and eatery that became the town's melting pot, thanks to its hospitable owner, Miss Bunny and her assistant Cindy.

In 1972, a music lover and visionary of Italian and Irish descent by the name of James Guercio had converted an old barn in the ghost town of Caribou into a state-of-the-art recording studio less than a mile from the Pioneer Inn. A diverse list of artists and musicians recorded albums at the Caribou Ranch studio, among them Carole King, Elton John, John Denver, Waylon Jennings, Frank Zappa, Michel Jackson, Rod Stewart,

Stevie Nicks and Jerry Lee Lewis, as well as a host of bands including Earth Wind and Fire, Chicago, and America. It was not uncommon to see Guercio's famous guests riding horses into town. Many recalled years later that their experience of recording in the mountain town was one of the highlights of their musical career. Elton John's 1974 album *Caribou* was recorded at and named after the studio. His remake single of "Lucy in the Sky with Diamonds" was recorded on a beautiful summer starlit night filled with shooting stars streaking across the Milky Way above the Continental Divide.

Dimitri lay down on a blanket with Spud curled up by his side and looked up into a night sky dense with clusters of stars. After a while, the stars he had seen first began to appear closer and more distant stars began to come into view. The last time Dimitri had experienced this visual phenomenon was in the night sky of the mountains in Lebanon, far away from the light pollution of cities.

The next morning, while exploring town, Dimitri noticed a flier posted on the community bulletin board by the food co-op, advertising a cabin for rent in the woods by the creek, in the neighboring town of Eldora.. It was just what Dimitri was hoping for. After meeting with the landlord, Fred, and paying him rent, Dimitri moved his belongings from his camper into the cabin, starting with Spud's cozy bed. After he had built his own bed, shelves, table and a couple of chairs, the cabin started to look and feel like home.

The first blissful two weeks working on his new home and taking hikes up the mountain paths with Spud while communing with nature, marked a special time of peace and serenity and formed a foundation on which to build his new life on. It was the first time he felt this way since before the war ten years ago in the mountains of Lebanon.

The next day, Dimitri packed a lunch and set out on foot with Spud, walking along the old dirt road into town while getting to know his neighbors along the way. Fred lived down the street in a cabin of his own making, with his dogs Buddy and Timber. Fred ran the recycling and refuse center for Nederland. He had organized the recycling scrap yard into dedicated areas: one for recycled doors, windows and building materials, and another with bicycles and skis that were still in good working order and were available for free. He also had a private stash of choice items that he saved for his friends: rare books for the professor, tools for his builder and craftsman friends, art and frames for the artists, and so on. He had built himself a cabin and a workspace from things others had thrown away.

The first time Dimitri had dropped off the rent and visited Fred's cabin, he was surprised and enthralled by the variety of artifacts and the collection of old cast-iron wood stoves. "How did you find all these things? Your cabin looks like a museum."

"It's one of the perks of working at the transfer station," said Fred. "Every so often, families from the city come up to the mountains to clear away the furnishings of a relative who died. They have no interest in the sentimental or material value of some of the things they get rid of. All they want to do is get the property listed and ready to sell. Sometimes they don't even take the time to show up in person. They just hire a company of strangers to empty out everything in the house and send it to the dump before the real estate agent lists the property for sale. Half of what they get rid of is useful and good. A few surprising gems show up every so often, like this antique Senate pot-belly stove from the 19th century that showed up last week."

Dimitri was inspired by Fred's example. He liked the concept of building a cabin with the many things people get rid of. Fred reminded Dimitri of one of his heroes, Dick Proenneke, who had built a cabin from scratch with hand tools in the Alaska wilderness. During Dimitri's first year in America, he saw a documentary film about Dick Proenneke in wood shop. Dick also reminded him a lot of Saleem, the old stonemason.

After walking on a trail through aspen groves, Dimitri and Spud arrived at the old part of town, which had a mix of old miner shacks and new, modern homes. One of the timber-frame homes on a corner lot had several unique mythological sculptures surrounding it. At the beginning of the walkway leading to the front door was a large iron sculpture of a minotaur archer, half horse and half man, drawing an archer's bow. Further up on a rock was a sculpture of a thinker contemplating a globe held in his hand. On the east side of the house were sculptures of a jazz horn section, next to a violin player, and above them on a hill was a Kokopelli playing a flute.

Throughout the yard were many abstract metal sculptures that looked like totem poles made of old tools, wrenches, picks, horseshoes, car parts, springs and scrap metal, cut and bent into shapes and then welded together. They were topped with a winged glass eyeball that reflected the sun's light.

While Dimitri was contemplating the sculpture of the minotaur, a man in blue overalls walked up with a limp and asked in a scratchy, smoky voice, "What do you think?"

"Very interesting minotaur," Dimitri said. The man nodded with a smile and introduced himself as John Marion Reynolds, home builder by day and metal sculpture artist by night and weekends. Dimitri introduced himself as a fellow welder and stone mason. The two talked shop and building before delving into the origins and meanings of the mythology represented in the sculptures.

"You're one of the few people that understand these sculptures," John said. "I had one of the old church ladies tell me they were weird and scary." letting out a loud, coarse laugh that reminded Dimitri of a pirate's laugh. Dimitri chuckled along with John. "Some people are scared of what they are not familiar with and don't understand," said Dimitri. John nodded in agreement.

*   *   *

Over the next few weeks, the two became friends as Dimitri stopped by on his regular walks with Spud into town to chat. John was a man of contrasts, born to a hard-working, hard-drinking, ambitious Texan father and a culturally refined and artistic Parisian mother. His parents had met in France during the Second World War and returned to Texas after getting married.

John had been a prolific sketcher since childhood. He took his pad and pencil with him everywhere he went, sketching street scenes, figures, faces, trees, leaves, vines, birds, insects and Whatever else caught his eye and interest. After graduating from high school in Texas, he spent some time at his French grandmother's apartment in Paris while attending Les Beaux-Arts de Paris. On his return, Texas, which boasts of being a place where everything is bigger, had paradoxically become too small for him. John, the young carpenter, artist and renaissance man, packed his truck with his tools and headed west to Colorado to seek a new creative and independent life of his own making.

There he established himself as a fine carpenter and builder of several timber-frame homes, one of which was for the mayor of his adopted home in Nederland.

There seemed to be a mythical, even divine mystique surrounding John and five other builders who worked with him when they restored a church in Boulder County's Fourmile Canyon. It was one of the early settler churches called The Little Church in The Pines, built in the late 1800s on a row of stones that had shifted over time and started to negatively affect the church's structure. John and his crew encased the church with an outer skeleton of lumber and lifted the whole church four feet off the ground with multiple 25-ton jacks. A new solid foundation was built underneath it before the church was settled back down gently and anchored to its foundation.

Years later, after an infamous flood washed away all the town's cabins and homes in Fourmile Canyon, the only structure that remained standing was The Little Church in The Pines, still resting on its solid foundation. The town's residents took that as a divine message that encouraged them to rebuild the town again around the church. Hiring John and his crew to build their new foundations.

One day, after receiving a commission from a well-known art critic, John, in his old torn, stitched, stained and patched work clothes, exclaimed with his usual self-deprecating humor, "Who knew? I guess I'm more refined than I look. But don't tell anyone; it's not good for my image." And then came one of his loud pirate laughs.

John didn't care about his image or what others thought of him. He wasn't caught up in the vanities and trappings of a conventional life. Fiercely independent, he had no tolerance for anyone who was not authentic. To John, it didn't matter what background you came from. Whether you were educated or not. What side of the tracks you grew up on. Your race or religion didn't concern him. The one thing that he held sacred was authenticity. He had a disdain for commercial and religious solicitors, salespeople, shapeshifters, fast talking slicksters and hypocrites with agendas. At the entrance to his home was a sign that read: *No soliciting, I have met Jesus, and I have everything I need. Please keep out.*

People felt lucky to be able to hire him, for his high level of workmanship but also for his character, recognizing that he was a rare and dying breed, a builder whose word and handshake were more solid and binding than a legal contract. With natural talent, a curious mind and a strong work ethic, he had mastered several trades. He once joked to Dimitri with a tweak of the old adage: "Jack of all trades, but master of none." Changing it to "Jack of all trades and a master of a few, but most importantly the master of the jack itself." He explained that to master the jack is to be the master of one's own being.

John had an independent, internally sound compass that guided him through a life of hard work, creativity and domestic bliss with his wife, Anne, and their two cats, along with the many diverse and loyal people who called him friend. An avid reader and fanatic collector of old blues vinyl albums, John, while physically lean and wiry, was a very heavy dude.

*　　*　　*

Walking on a bridge across Boulder Creek, Dimitri and Spud came across the Wolf Tongue Mine, an industrial ghost town that had been an engineering marvel in its heyday. The now abandoned mine had been one of the country's top producers of tungsten, a metal in high demand during the Second World War. Tungsten mixed with iron created the hardened steel casings of the Sherman tanks that rolled across Europe and were instrumental in bringing an end to the war.

Now the mine, along with its rusty machines and tattered conveyor belts stood silent, as if in mourning for a bygone era. The silence was punctuated by a crow's caws, rattles and clicks, while an occasional wind gust propelled the rusty ventilation fans to turn, letting out a metal-on-metal high pitch sound even after all these years. The wind whistled through the giant structure's dilapidated windows, that let out creaking sounds from the rusty iron hinges.

Walking through the Wolf Tongue Mine's ghost town, Dimitri and Spud came across two large, fully intact warehouses that seemed to have been restored and well maintained. A faint sound of a mallet tapping a chisel could be heard coming from the rusty orange warehouse at the farthest edge of the mine.

"Come on, Spud, let's take a look."

Approaching the open sliding barn doors, Dimitri saw a man wielding a wood chisel and mallet, chipping away at a sculpture of a horse. Behind him were rows of animal sculptures, including an elephant, camel, fox, hare, cheetah, bear, deer, goose, rooster, fish, frog, cow, dog, donkey and an assortment of other whimsical creatures.

"Good evening!" Dimitri called out to announce his presence.

"Good evening, welcome, come on in," replied the sculpture artist, who introduced himself as Harrison.

"I feel like I'm entering Noah's ark, Dimitri said. The large barn indeed looked like a ship. It housed cast-iron gears and mechanical parts in one area and large timbers that had been honed, treated and stacked in another. "What are you building?" he asked.

"I've been sculpting animals in wood for a carousel that I hope to build in town. Say, that's a healthy stout dog you got there."

"That's Spud. A Pitbull terrier mix. He's friendly and sweet. He's a good boy."

Just as Dimitri got those words out, Spud headed towards one of Harrison's sculptures and peed on it, then headed to another sculpture of a cheetah and began to growl at it.

"I'm sorry. I'll clean up," Dimitri said, embarrassed.

"Oh, don't worry about it," Harrison replied, laughing. "I guess it's a compliment that Spud sees my sculptures as real. Are you visiting?"

"I've been on a road trip from Seattle."

"That's a long trip. Interesting Seattle accent you have."

The two laughed.

"I'm originally from Lebanon."

"I thought maybe you were. I have a good friend I went to school with years ago, Bassam Khoury. His parents were from Lebanon. His mother made the best Lebanese food, kibbe, tabouli, baba ghanouj, fatoosh, all of it."

Dimitri was happily surprised that Harrison was familiar with his culture. He felt comfortable telling him about his journey from the old country to Seattle and the road trip to Nederland. He was impressed to learn how much Harrison knew about Lebanon. People tended to have simple stereotypical ideas of the region that were sensationalized by the media.

"You get a lot of snow up in the mountains there, don't you?"

"Yes, over five meters some winters."

"Wow! That's over fifteen feet."

"We have orographic lifting like you have here in Truckee, California with the Pacific Ocean. Our mountains get a lot of moisture from the Mediterranean Sea. It's a similar thing."

Harrison seemed to know not only about the Middle Eastern conflicts that made the news, but also about the geography, history and the culture. It wasn't every day that Dimitri met someone who could quote from Khalil Gibran's poems.

The two enjoyed their conversations whenever Dimitri and Spud occasionally passed by Harrison's workshop during their evening walk after dinner through the ghost town of Wolf Tongue Mine. The ghost town reminded Dimitri of downtown Beirut during the war, when he would patrol with his comrades through abandoned, desolate buildings.

Over time, Dimitri learned that he and Harrison had seen their lives shaped by similar experiences. At 18, the energetic, bright and naive young Harrison had joined the Marine Corps during the Vietnam War. His sharp mind and interest in other cultures was an asset that he developed to serve his country as an interpreter. Harrison hoped to be a facilitator and a bridge between the two cultures and seemed to those who knew him more like a priest than a warrior.

In 1967, when the war in Vietnam took a turn for the worse and America became entrenched in the quagmire of the war, the Marines needed to replenish their losses on the front lines with new live bodies. That's when Harrison and his company were sent out to a base on the farthest reaches of the front lines. *Con Thien*, in Vietnamese, means the hill of angels. The area had infamously earned the grim nickname "Hell on the Hill of Angels" It was there, while defending the Con Thien base, that his company came under heavy attack by the North Vietnamese.

Harrison saw comrades and close friends blown up, many shredded to pieces, all around him. Harrison himself was seriously wounded and flown out by helicopter to be put back together again. During his stay in the hospital, he struggled to distance himself from the darkness by escaping mentally to a peaceful place. His sister had sent him a small portable music box that played Chopin's "Tristesse" every time he wound it up, which he did often. The music gave him comfort while he imagined a carousel turning to the music in a peaceful mountain meadow.

That feeling and image stayed with him. After the war ended, he decided to build the carousel of his imagination in honor of his fallen comrades, and in doing so to create something that would spread joy for generations to come.

Harrison began to carve the large wooden sculptures of animals that he planned to assemble on the restored mechanism of a retired 1910 Looff carousel, which would turn to the music of a 1913 Wurlitzer band organ.

Harrison cut, carved and sanded for countless hours, working late in his workshop, to realize his dream. It became a nightly meditative ritual after having supper with his family.

After twenty years of work, the carousel was ready to be assembled. The Carousel of Happiness, as it became known, was built with the help of the many local carpenters, masons, engineers and community volunteers who pitched in to make it a reality. The carousel was filled with a menagerie of 56 colorful, whimsical and magical creatures rotating to upbeat, festive organ music while bringing joy, cheer, giggles and laughter to young and old alike.

Harrison's journey was inspirational to Dimitri and reminded him of his old mentor, David, in Seattle, who used to say, "Life is made of many chapters. Don't get stuck on the same chapter all your life." Harrison had overcome the darkness of his past by creating beautiful things that brought joy to others.

*   *   *

Dimitri and Spud headed further up the hill overlooking Wolf Tongue Mine, where a shipping container was the home of Doug, the knife sharpener. Doug had arrived at the mountain town a year earlier, along with his shipping container that he made into a tiny home and workshop. He established himself by first sharpening two of the local grill's commercial knives in exchange for dinner. From there, knowledge of his skill and workmanship spread by word of mouth. It was enough to keep him busy, but not too much to take away from his favorite pastime, fishing.

Doug was also a handyman with a good working knowledge of general house repairs. He was a sentimental time traveler and dreamer. A constant drifter strumming folksy and bluesy tunes on his guitar, with a set of skills and enough of a work ethic that allowed him to pursue such a life without becoming destitute.

If anyone asked what he wished for, he would say: a good woman to raise a family with. Tragically, that dream could never be reconciled with the strong pull he always felt to move on to a new place, to meet new people, sing a few songs, have a few laughs and more than a few beers before moving on to the next town on his great adventure. It was an aimless quest for happiness and meaning that alcohol always seemed to get in the way of.

Dimitri enjoyed talking shop with Doug occasionally and listening to one of his tunes. They even went fishing.

One day, when Spud and Dimitri had been visiting with Harrison, they crossed the bridge over Boulder Creek and climbed up the hill into town and came upon an empty space underneath a familiar ponderosa pine. Doug's shipping container was not there anymore. They stood there for a while, puzzled, looking at the empty space that had been Doug's home. The imprints from the container where still visible on the earth where it once stood.

An elderly woman came walking up to Dimitri and Spud from the house down the street next to the Good Karma Center.

"Good morning, Madam," Dimitri said. He always got funny reactions when he respectfully addressed someone in such a way. Some were pleased and familiar with his formal decorum, while with others it wasn't clear if they were puzzled or offended. In America, it turned out, *Madam* was a word sometimes associated with being the boss lady at a brothel.

"Good morning, young man. How is Spud today?" Spud was wagging his tail enthusiastically as she approached. He liked the woman, who always petted him and talked to him.

"What happened here? Is Doug still around?" Dimitri asked.

Giving him a disappointed look, she said, "Well, this morning a truck backed up to the container and placed it onto its bed. Doug was sitting in the passenger seat as the truck drove off. We waved to each other, and that's about it. He's an interesting feller, that Doug. Sorry to see him go so abruptly. I had hoped for him to settle here. He worked on my fence and fixed the roof. I thought we had a good rapport and that he would let me know if he was leaving. I guess a drifter does what a drifter has to do.

"The bright young lady geologist up the hill and Doug seemed to have taken a shine to each other. I thought they were suitably matched. It's just as well, I guess. She needs someone more grounded."

*   *   *

Dimitri likewise was sad to see Doug leave. He and Spud headed into town for a few supplies, with the sound of horse hoofs in a slow four beat gait and two riders coming up behind them.. The horses were obviously familiar with dogs and unfazed by Spud, who came up to them and exchanged nose nuzzles. Evidently good messages were exchanged, and the animals hung out outside the grocery store together while Dimitri picked up a dozen eggs.

On their way back to the cabin they came across an older woman with white, braided hair standing transfixed behind an easel, a paintbrush in her hand. Dimitri took a wide turn to avoid disturbing the artist as she gazed at the creek where its water was channeled through large boulders with highlights of sunshine reflecting off them. But the ever-curious Spud went straight up to her.

"I'm sorry, my dog is both curious and friendly," Dimitri said apologetically.

"Oh, no worries, I love dogs."

"Good boy," said the artist while extending her hand out for Spud to approach. She patted his head and gently talked to him; words Dimitri couldn't hear over the babbling sounds of the creek. But they must have been sweet, as Spud continued to wag his tail.

"Beautiful painting," he exclaimed.

"Oh, thank you. It gets me out here in communion with nature."

*   *   *

Willow lived a quiet, independent life of an artist in the neighboring mountain town of Ward. The town had been the site of gold mining once, hidden in the recesses of a ravine surrounded by natural wonders and endless trails meandering through the Roosevelt National Forest and

Brainard Lake.

There was no sign welcoming visitors to Ward. There was a sign however in a front yard of a house at the entrance of the town that read: "The more you know, the less you need." The town's residents seemed to be independent and eccentric characters. At one time, the town had the highest per capita number of PhDs in the country, mostly philosophers, artists and poets.

This was no exclusive gated community. Most residents lived in cabins and shacks. Willow described her town as a live-and-let-live town. "No one tells you what to do, and you're okay as long as you're respectful, considerate, tread lightly and don't bother anyone." The town had a sheriff by the name of Fuzzy Bob and two deputies, Skinny Pete and Tiny Bowers, who was anything but tiny. Tiny Bowers ran the Harley-Davidson repair shop in town and was also the fire chief. The town had no street names and no traffic lights. The Ward Library was a remarkable building and the centerpiece of town, housing an extensive collection of books covering a wide range of genres and subjects.

A cabin in the mountains

As he'd been told early on, Dimitri indeed found all these Colorado small towns to be filled with independent, diverse, eccentric and colorful characters. By now he had decided to put roots down in the mountains and give it a go. So, he headed to Boulder's municipal building and inquired about starting his own stonemasonry business. After filling out the necessary forms, he introduced himself and established a cordial working relationship with the local family-owned quarries in the nearby town of Lyons.

There was an abundance of raw building material for his trade in Lyons, which was known for its unique red stone from the Permian period, 260 million years ago. The beautiful red stone is considered the hardest sandstone in the world but is soft in comparison to the limestone Dimitri had grown up working with in the old country.

After a trip to McGuckin's hardware store in Boulder to retool, Dimitri was ready for his first commercial stonemasonry job in Colorado. He was hired to build two stone columns, which would accommodate a custom iron gate John had been commissioned to build for an entrance of a house in the foothills of Boulder. After completing the columns on time and below budget, he was given a new job building a retaining wall and stone steps. Dimitri's reputation for quality, old-world masonry spread by word of mouth, and in a short time he had more job offers than he could accept.

Dimitri was happy to be working with stone again and began to feel truly settled in his new cabin in the mountains only 15 minutes away from a city with a well-educated, well-traveled and worldly population, who appreciated the durability and old-world esthetics of stone masonry. There was plenty of work to make a good living and make a life for himself and Spud.

He remembered the old stonemason Saleem telling him years ago that whenever he found himself at a crossroad in life, "Don't fall into the trap of indulgently taking time off for too long to think about things. Instead, stay involved doing good, honest, meaningful work, and remain in the river of daily life that only moves forward. That's when the right answers, good people and good ideas will present themselves to you."

Boulder had an interesting demographic that included brilliant scientists, artists, spiritual seekers, intellectuals, athletes training at high altitude, and slackers. The driving forces of the city were Ball Aerospace, the National Center for Atmospheric Research, IBM and the University of Colorado.

There were large numbers of spiritual seekers from around the country who would visit Boulder to spend time at the renowned Shambala Center, a cultural institution dedicated to creating an enlightened society that would embody bravery, compassion and confidence in basic goodness.

The city also had a hippie-chic vibe, many were trust-funders who fancied themselves as free-spirited gypsies while living in million-dollar homes. This superficial cool style was a fantasy people of privilege could afford to indulge in without the hardships of a real nomad's life. Among that demographic were several "trustafarians" that raged against the machine while getting their check each month from the very machine they raged against, or at least the machine their parents worked for that afforded them to live a carefree life while pretending to be social revolutionaries.

For all its diverse and genuinely interesting population, Boulder had its share of self-absorbed, self-indulgent people living in a bubble of entitlement. This again made Dimitri think of Saleem's values, and how immune he has been from the whims, fads, distractions and illusions of the modern world. Saleem was grounded and united with nature, while maintaining a deep commitment to his family, community and work. There was something basic, simple and true about the old stonemason that was as solid and timeless as the mountains themselves.

*   *   *

Every dawn, Dimitri and Spud would start the new day with a walk along Boulder Creek before heading to work.

Those morning walks offered a sense of joy and contentment, giving Dimitri a chance to let go of his human thoughts and ideas while strolling along Boulder Creek; there, he and Spud were in tune with their natural surroundings, and in tune with the bird's song, the buzz of a bee flying by, the sound of the rippling creek and trickling water flowing over the rocks, the rising sun's rays peering through the evergreen trees and shimmered across the water's surface, with the scent of the morning dew. Their walks together were moments of pure bliss. While most people worship in churches, mosques and temples, Dimitri worshiped in nature, and it was there he felt in communion with God.

Walking along the creek, Spud would tilt his head to amplify the sound of the bird's song while his moist nose picked up countless messages. Every so often, he would glance at Dimitri as if to confirm that both were in on this special time together. Dimitri silently smiled back at Spud, the dog wagging his tail in response to this confirmation before he resumed his sensory investigation in complete focus and union with nature. Spud accompanied Dimitri to all his jobs and became known as "the building inspector" for constantly coming up to various tradespeople to greet them and get patted while he inspected their work, wagging his tail. Everyone loved Spud and got a chuckle when he came to visit them. Spud and Dimitri were together 24 hours a day, seven days a week. Their inseparability was rooted in love, loyalty and the sacred nature of their simple, true and trusting relationship.

Dimitri became part of the mountain community and, before long, felt at home with its many characters. There, he found a new perspective, a new understanding, and deeper meaning in the simple truths of life. While the Rockies were different from his beloved Mount Lebanon, there was a similarity with the independent individuals who lived in a collective community spirit. There is something sound, timeless and true wherever the air is fresh, the water is clean, and the people are without pretenses.

Athena

One morning when Spud and Dimitri were on their walk, they saw a woman approaching at a distance with a dog by her side. Dimitri noticed she was sweet and patient with her gray-muzzled old dog. She patiently let the dog investigate the edges of the path, sniffing for clues as to who and what had passed by recently. The dog's investigation was carried out with the meticulous focus, interest and patience of an elderly person reading a newspaper.

As they got closer, Dimitri realized how beautiful the woman was. She had soulful brown eyes that twinkled with warmth and depth. She wore no makeup, and her long, dark hair was brushed back into a simple ponytail, with a cap and visor adorning her head. She looked confident and comfortable with herself in a way that was very appealing. She walked calmly yet with a sense of awareness, purpose and direction.

"Good morning," Dimitri greeted her.

"Good morning."

Dimitri stood mesmerized for an awkward moment, mutely beaming a smile. There was a mutual attraction that the dogs seemed to pick up on. Both had a funny look, as if they knew something their humans were not aware of yet. The two dogs wagged their tails vigorously before joyfully running off together, thrashing along the creek's banks in a game of chase and tag.

"Lucy seems to really like your dog," the woman said. "I haven't seen her act like this in years."

"Spud is a good dog. He's a gentle soul. He seems to really like your dog as well."

Dimitri introduced himself telling her he had recently moved from Seattle and was renting the Wren cabin farther down the creek.

"Welcome to the community. I think you'll like it here," she said, introducing herself as Athena.

"Spud and I take our walk by the creek every morning before heading for work. We haven't seen you along the creek before."

"My schedule at work changed. I've been on a stretch of night shifts at the hospital, but now I'm working days and have started a new morning routine taking Lucy on a walk before heading to work."

"That's what Spud and I do. It's a good start of the day."

"They are wonderful companions, aren't they?"

"They sure are. I think it's Lucy that takes me for a walk instead of me taking her."

The two laughed before the conversation evolved from introductions and pleasantries to a more substantive conversation about their lives and how they had come to be living in this small mountain town in Colorado. There was something familiar about Athena, though the two had never met before. They both felt an instant sense of ease and familiarity with each other. Spud and Lucy came back running from the creek, shaking their heads vigorously and transferring the wiggles all the way back to the tips of their tails while dowsing their humans with water from the creek. The shaking ended with them both looking wide-eyed at their humans, their tongues hanging out in an ecstatic expression of joy, as if to say, "Do you see this? Isn't this great?" Then off they went, for another round of splashing in the creek.

Athena and Dimitri continued down the path together, breathing in the misty cool air of dawn while exchanging stories, thoughts and ideas.

Athena and Dimitri began meeting daily for their morning walks and then started to take longer hikes together with their dogs on the weekend. There was a natural compatible energy and rhythm between them. While they enjoyed having conversations, they also enjoyed the quiet and peace of just being present together in nature.

The strong attraction and affection they each felt for each other blossomed and grew with each day they spent together. They also began to develop a strong emotional trust. For Dimitri, meeting Athena felt different than anything he'd experienced before. He instinctively felt this was one of those major connections in life. There was something beautiful, bright, warm, earthy and true about her. Being with Athena made him expand his lungs, stand straight and breathe more deeply.

For Athena, Dimitri was an interesting change as well. He was gregarious, warm, earnest, gentle, and with a strong backbone. He was a bit old fashioned, which was a refreshing change for Athena who was disillusioned by the single scene. Dimitri was an open book. What you saw is what you got. And Athena liked what she saw. They both had a social sensibility that belonged to a different era, considered old-fashioned by co-workers and peers who spent their free time drinking and attending parties, while Athena saved lives at the hospital and found joy in music, art and working on her projects at home with her trusty dog Lucy during her time off. Dimitri as well was dedicated to his work as a stonemason and spent his time off with his dog Spud, his camera and tripod hiking in the Rocky Mountains.

Athena had a curious mind, a strong spirit and an appreciation for the past, while living her life in the present with dreams and hopes for the future. Dimitri recognized that she was a self-actualized person that had the full spectrum of knowing who she was, where she came from, where she is in the present and what she hoped for and aspired to in the future.

While Dimitri's stonemasonry work was physically demanding, Athena's 12 hour shifts at the hospital were mentally and emotionally taxing.

*   *   *

Dimitri was always there for Athena, with a sensitive ear, thoughtful mind, and an open heart. He had always been grateful to healthcare workers. Not only because of his beloved grandmother Teta, the matriarch of the family who was a nurse and embodied all the qualities of a true caregiver.

But also, the doctors and nurses that treated, stitched, and helped put him back together again on a number of occasions.

Dimitri reflected on how they are a gift from heaven to humanity. They have a strong, warm and compassionate heart that brightens the darkest days while they dispense health, hope, self-respect, care and compassion.

They are kind and caring sentinel souls who keep a vigil over their patients, putting the needs of the patient before their own. Hard working, strong, swift and calm while witnessing miracles, life and death. Caregiving is much more than a job. It's a calling and a profession of skill delivered with empathy, compassion, a gentle touch and a caring smile.

While advancements in diagnostics and even surgery is increasingly reliant on state-of-the-art machines, the hardest and most meaningful work of taking care of patients will always remain in the realm of the healthcare worker's humanity and dedication.

*   *   *

Dimitri remembered the first time Athena invited him to lunch. He picked a bouquet of wildflowers for her along the way and showed up ten minutes early. She came to the door wearing jeans and a flannel shirt.

"Welcome, come on in," she said. Spud and Lucy were equally happy to see each other, with tails wagging in a blur of excitement. Walking into Athena's house, Dimitri noticed it had the warmth of a home. There were many things she'd had a hand in creating, ceramics, drawings, and paintings, as well as plants she nurtured. Dimitri had noticed her strong maternal bond to Lucy, which he found endearing and mirrored his feelings towards Spud. It was another positive confirmation of their compatibility.

Dimitri had always found it strange and cold when he entered someone's home where there was nothing in it that the person living there had made or nurtured. Instead, such homes were filled with items that had been purchased, often merely for show. They were things intended to show wealth or prestige. But to Dimitri they showed a lack of depth, imagination, creativity and warmth.

"I made us tabouli," Athena said.

"That's my favorite. How did you know?"

"I know what's good," she said confidently, with a sly smile.

Athena had set up her chop saw on the porch; she was working on framing and trimming her windows. There was something very appealing about her hands-on, can-do attitude, which was grounded and visible both in her daily work as a healthcare worker helping others and, in her hobbies, which involved creating and nurturing.

"I didn't know you were into carpentry."

"My father built our family home when I was a child. I loved spending time with him, and over the years he taught me how to build things, starting with bird houses and bird feeders."

"That's really useful and nice; sounds like a great dad."

"He is. I was always his little buddy growing up. My friends' fathers called their daughters *princess*. He never called me that. He called me many other names of endearment, like sunshine, sweetheart and love, but never princess. His socialist outlook didn't see that as a compliment. I remember causing a controversy as a kid when I presented a paper in school titled "Princesses are lame.""

Dimitri laughed out loud. "I guess you had more sense as a kid than many adults do. I see you've sanded and finished the trim. It looks nice with the warm stain and matte finish."

"Thank you!"

Far from being born with a silver spoon in her mouth, Athena had worked at her family's restaurant from a young age and helped her aging Greek immigrant grandparents after school. Though they were now deceased, their portraits hung on the wall in her living room. She had drawn them with charcoal on paper while visiting them on Christmas during her college years. Athena's love, respect, and reverence for her grandparents and family was an endearing trait, that was another sign of Athena and Dimitri's sensibility, outlook and compatibility with each other.

*   *   *

After lunch, Athena asked "You want to come with me and check on Zeus?"

"Sure! Is this some sort of mythological riddle, wrapped in a mystery, inside an enigma?"

Athena smirked. "He's a horse I take care of and sponsor at the Four Winds Horse Sanctuary."

"I would love to meet him."

The sanctuary was owned and run by her friend Julie, an impressive woman with a big heart whose life mission was rescuing horses, along with dogs, cats and an assortment of other creatures. Athena headed towards a stall holding a large, tan-colored draft horse she had rescued and boarded two years ago, after his owner, Bufford, died. Bufford's son William had come up to the mountains from the city and was interested in selling the farm as quickly as possible so he could return to his busy life with his neurotic wife and over-scheduled children. He did not have the interest or patience to come up with a more imaginative solution for the farm animals than to sell them for slaughter.

William, like many men, was both admirable and pathetic. Admirable for putting his family first. Pathetic for drinking the Kool-Aid of conformity in a job he hated. What he loved best was a football team whose statistics he was more knowledgeable about than what was going on around him politically and socially and how that would affect him, his family, and the world. It wasn't clear whether he really had no idea or if this was a self-imposed state of numbness, one where he had deliberately pruned himself of awareness, creativity, and compassion. Either way, he was no more than a cog in the corporate machinery. By conventional standards of conformity, William was doing well. He was a man with a plan, where everything was scheduled, compartmentalized, and efficient.

Julie caught wind of William's plan through the local grapevine, over breakfast at the Pioneer Inn. With Athena's help, she moved to save the old workhorse Zeus and a goat named Willie.

It was as if Zeus knew that Athena had saved his life, or at least made it better. As soon as he saw her, he started to whinny softly, which then gently turned into a deep-bass guttural, grumbly and bubbly sound of happiness and affection.

"Where do you ride Zeus?" asked Dimitri.

"I don't. I just like to take care of him. He likes taking walks together in the meadow sometimes. But otherwise, he is free to run with his friends at Four Winds. Horses are born free until we humans use them as beasts of burden, transportation, war and entertainment. Zeus worked hard all his life. I just want him to live out his remaining years as free as possible and unmanipulated."

Dimitri had never thought of it that way. He had always seen horses depicted in grandiose settings that were even further magnified in his imagination. At church during his childhood, there was Saint George on a horse slaying the dragon. At school, in history class, he was fascinated by the stories of medieval knights in shining armor on top of their magnificent beasts. On occasional weekends, he went with his cousins and uncle to the racetrack for a shot of adrenalin, watching and hearing the rumbling stampede of hoofs vibrating the earth as the high-strung, spirited Arabian horses charged towards the finish line.

Dimitri and Athena both loved the magnificent creatures. But Athena had a different perspective and a true, deeper love and appreciation of them. "It's a human trait to use things. It's even considered a measure of intelligence in our world. I have made it a point not to use anything with a living spirit and instead try to nurture it," she explained. Athena was introducing Dimitri to a new way of seeing things that he had not considered before. He knew she was beginning to occupy a place deep in his heart.

Athena loved spending time with Zeus, cleaning his stall, shoveling sawdust into a wheelbarrow and making him a fresh bed for the evening. "This is my exercise after work," she said while mixing him a special bucket of oats, barley and molasses, a treat he enjoyed while she brushed him and sweetly talked to him. Their conversations seemed partly verbal and partly telepathic or emotional, communication that Zeus seemed to understand and respond to affectionately, with contented eyes, gentle nudges and finally by placing his giant head to rest on her shoulder in a sort of horse hug, while she petted his warm muzzle. "I love the smell of horse breath. It smells both sweet and musky."

A woman who understands and loves her horse and takes good care of him is a special person who understands how sensitive the beast is, Dimitri reflected. He, in turn, trusts and loves her.

For the first time in his life, Dimitri felt fully understood by a woman and not just superficially desired for ulterior motives. He'd experienced being an exotic experience by rebellious, young women from conservative families. Or to bolster a girl's liberal coolness when she showed up to a party with a foreigner. Or as a protector against an abusive ex-boyfriend. Or for having made a sum of money when he sold his shares of the fitness equipment company. Dimitri's relationships in the new world had always seemed to involve an ulterior motive.

It hadn't all been bad; in fact, it wasn't bad at all. After all, he was a young man in his twenties and didn't mind the attention. But he did long for a true love that has the full spectrum of passion, warmth, affection, depth, honesty, trust and fidelity. He had been a hopeless romantic, in love with the idea of being in love but never really finding it ... until now.

*   *   *

Dimitri invited his friends to a summer barbecue at his cabin by the creek. There was something for everyone. Beer, brats, shish kabobs, kofta, vegetables and onions grilled over red-hot coals. There was even seasoned grilled tofu for his friends from Boulder. Athena made a Tabouli with parsley, burghul, tomatoes, olive oil and lemon juice.

The couple set up chairs and brought out the coolers on the porch. Soon guests arrived. Matthew, Heidi and their kids Jasper and Miles set up a slackline between two trees and began to balance and walk across it. Kevin and his wife Jen showed up after having been gone for months. Kevin on a photojournalism assignment, and Jen with the UNICEF relief agency. Susie and her girlfriend Dorian set up a badminton net and floated around like joyful butterflies on a sunny summer's day. Fred hammered metal stakes into the ground for the iron horseshoe toss, as more guests showed up while Herbie played his slide guitar. "This is for you, Dimitri," he called out as he played a tune from surf guitar pioneer Dick Dale, who was born in Boston to a Lebanese father and Polish mother. Drawing on Middle Eastern musical scales and experimenting with reverb, the man known as the "king of surf guitar" had influenced Jimi Hendrix, Pete Townshend, Brian May and others.

Everyone knew Herbie, who was a contributing musician on Friday nights at the Pioneer Inn as well as serving as the town's rural postman, a position held in high regard by the townsfolk, especially those living in the farther reaches of the mountain community. They relied on Herbie to stay connected, with a letter from family or a *Time* or *Newsweek* magazine to keep them informed of what was happening out there in the "real world", while reinforcing their gratitude for not having to live in it.

Herbie joined the Navy in his youth and visited the world's ports before completing his education and returning to the mountains. He and Dimitri had become friends through their common interest in stone. For over 15 years, Herbie had collected stones he came across on his delivery routes. Every year new stones and boulders would collect at the bottom of hills along the edges of the mountain roads. And over the years, stone by stone, Herbie had built a dwelling of them in the woods next to his log cabin.

Herbie was a self-taught stonemason. Dimitri filled the gaps of knowledge and gave him tips on stonemasonry and the various formulas of mortar used for different applications. Herbie in turn introduced Dimitri to the Japanese art of stone appreciation known as *Suiseki*, the meditative practice of walking along a creek in the woods while looking for small, naturally formed stones selected for their shape, balance, simplicity and tranquility.

Looking around at his friends at the barbeque, with Athena by his side, Dimitri knew that he found his home in the new world. He also knew he had found his life partner and wife.

Into the future

The universal desire of all living things to find their counterpart and perpetuate their species belongs less to the realm of rational thought than to nature itself and the great mystery of life.

Anyone who has seen a bird spend every hour of daylight shuttling back and forth to its nest to feed it's offspring recognizes the deep instinct of selfless dedication it takes to raise a healthy new generation that will be able to fly on its own and create its own future.

That nurturing instinct manifests in different ways for humans. Some dedicate themselves to their families, some to other living beings, and others to a just cause they feel will benefit humanity. At the core, it's the same evolution of spiritual maturity and outlook, where another being becomes more important than one's own self.

Dimitri and Athena, along with their dogs Spud and Lucy, lived a year of domestic bliss together before getting married. The first winter after they wed, their cabin was blanketed in snow. With provisions sufficient for a snowbound week, Dimitri built a fire that cast a warm orange glow through the cabin. Spud and Lucy curled up next to each other, while their humans sat on a couch, gazing out the window into the heavens. Dimitri held Athena close as she leaned back against him, their fingers intertwined and clasped gently over her abdomen, sending warmth and love to a new generation about to enter the world.

Both understood they were not just embarking on another phase or chapter of their lives but starting a whole new book. Until now, they'd been guided by their upbringings and life experiences, but this was uncharted territory. They had each other's trust and support and were united in their belief that their total dedication would be to their child and family.

Every phase in life has its time to be fulfilled. In youth, every strong, independent spirit asserts, "I've got to be me." Some never outgrow that sentiment. Luckily, Dimitri and Athena had evolved into self-actualized people who knew who they were before bringing a new life into the world. The days of personal quests and ambitions—some noble, some necessary, and some foolish—were left in the past as they looked forward to this most important time in their lives: creating a family together, with their eyes, minds, and hearts open to all the wonders, joys, sacrifices, and challenges ahead while walking courageously in step with each other before taking flight into the future.